A Voyage of Vengeance

~A Court of Mystery Novella~

Book Three

Sarah E. Burr

Other books by Sarah E. Burr

The Court of Mystery series

The Ducal Detective
A Feast Most Foul
A Voyage of Vengeance
A Summit in Shadow
Throne of Threats
Paradise Plagued
Burdened Bloodline
Sovereign Sieged
Crown of Chaos
Harrowed Heir
Ravaged Reign
Innocence Imprisoned
Ardent Ascension
Eternal Empire

More Cozy Mysteries by Sarah

Trending Topic Mysteries
Glenmyre Whim Mysteries
Book Blogger Mysteries

www.saraheburr.com

A brief history…

Centuries ago, the corrupt and powerful priests of the Ancient Faith lorded over the continent. Poverty and sickness ravaged the world, forcing a faction of rebels to rise up and overthrow these tyrants preaching in the name of silent gods. The leaders of this movement, known in the annals of history as the Rebirth, proclaimed the realm would no longer answer to nameless demons and gods, but to the virtues of bravery, humility, kindness, and intelligence. Under these Virtues, the world would once again flourish. Sealing their pact, these newly anointed leaders drank the dew of the fabled kingsleaf flower, ensuring their offspring would be marked as the divine protectors of this new era with their royal eyes.

Welcome to the Realm of Virtues.

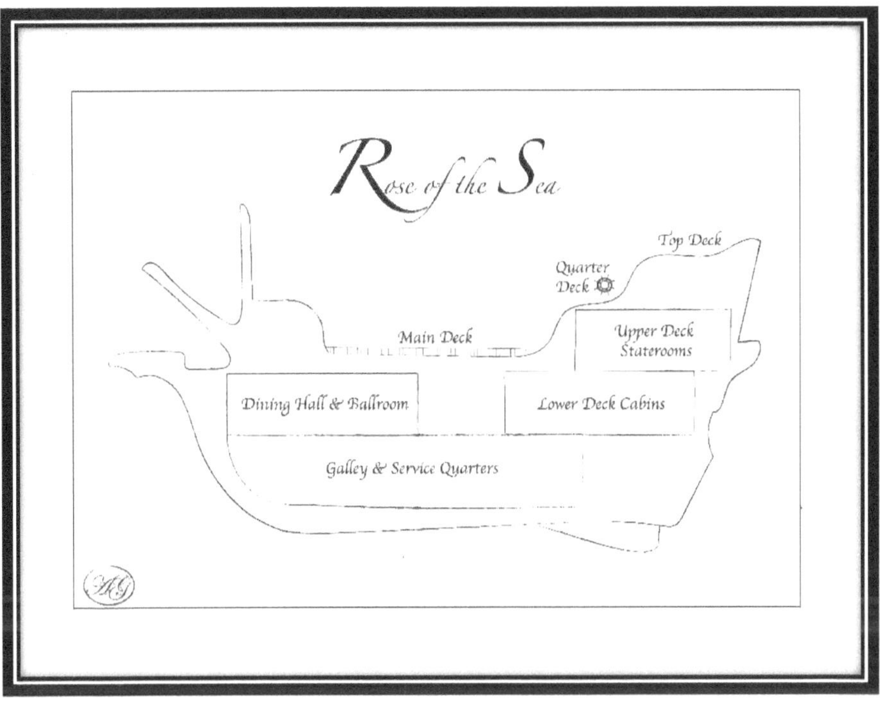

Rose of the Sea
Top Deck
Quarter Deck
Main Deck
Upper Deck Staterooms
Dining Hall & Ballroom
Lower Deck Cabins
Galley & Service Quarters

Chapter One

The smell of salty sea air assaulted her nostrils, an abrupt cough stuttering from her parched throat. Foolishly, she had gulped down her water supply early on during the bumpy carriage ride, forgetting the age-old rule that the royal caravan is forbidden to stop and accept offerings along its route. She would just have to wait until they arrived at the port, where her drinking water would be thoroughly tested for poison. There was a time in Jax's life where these precautionary measures seemed a bit overzealous, but as the last living heir to the Saphire throne, her safety was of the utmost importance.

"I won't tell anyone if you want a sip of mine, Your Grace." Uma extended a slender arm, offering her canteen, the water slushing teasingly inside.

Pausing only for a moment, Duchess Jacqueline Arienta Xavier gratefully took the gift and chugged its contents. Thankfully, her lady's maid had the restraint to ration her provisions for the long ride to the Duchy of Tandora. Across from her, Uma's petite figure sat at rapt attention, her common-folk brown eyes taking in the wondrous landscapes passing outside their windows. For most of the journey, Jax's enjoyment came from watching Uma react to the lush rainforests and wildlife, as the young woman had never seen such exotic sights. Years had passed since Jax had been to the coastal province, and she, too, was delighted by the scenery on display.

"I never dreamed the world could be so green and vibrant." Uma sighed in awe, her eyes sparkling with eagerness. She turned and gave her sovereign a smile, silently expressing her gratitude once more for the opportunity to ride inside the ducal carriage. With its large, curved windows, it offered a perfect view of the foreign land.

"Just wait until we reach the port town, where you'll see how big and blue the sea is!" Jax teased, sinking into the plush cushions behind her. As much as she tried to conceal it, the Duchess was bursting with excitement of her own. It had been years since she'd seen Carriena, one of her closest friends from her days at the Academy. Lady Carriena was the only daughter of Duke DeLacqua, and their shared royal heritage forever bound their friendship. Since graduation, the two had kept in touch with frequent letters, their responsibilities never allowing the right time to coordinate a visit. Now, the Virtues had finally aligned, giving Jax the perfect reason to see her longtime friend.

She pulled a thick scroll from a nearby satchel, unrolling the parchment. Golden ink shimmered in the afternoon sun as Jax's amethyst eyes, the mark of her royal heritage, scanned the sweeping invitation. *Rose of the Sea* was set to make its maiden voyage home to the island duchy of Isla DeLacqua, where it would make berth for the remainder of its days.

The three-masted ship, constructed by a famed Tandorian artisan from the region's strongest trees, was said to be the most luxurious craft to ever take to the water. Duke DeLacqua commissioned the masterpiece himself, a gift for his beloved daughter's twenty-eighth birthday. Using the ship's christening as an opportunity to forge stronger relations with the mainland duchies, the Duke had extended invitations to various individuals throughout the Realm of Virtues, welcoming them to embark on the inaugural journey with Lady Carriena.

Jax, of course, accepted the Duke's request almost immediately, welcoming the chance to escape Saphire for a little respite. It had been nearly a year since she'd assumed the throne after her parents' tragic deaths, and her time had been consumed with her royal duties. She longed for the carefree days of her youth, or as carefree as they had seemed to be now that she was Duchess. The past months had been filled with obligation after obligation, with never a moment's rest. How her beloved father managed to make his leadership look so effortless all those years vexed her to her very core. So, when Saphire's invitation arrived, much to High Courtier Jaquobie's chagrin, she personally accepted.

Word had reached her that she was the only sovereign set to embark on *Rose of the Sea*. Jaquobie's messengers had reported other duchies were sending emissaries of the crown, not wanting to risk their own heads on a ship's debut at sea. Her many advisors insisted she send someone in her stead, but she waved away their concerns. She loved being out on the water. When she was a young girl and her father brought her to Isla DeLacqua for the first time, she begged to be allowed to stay on the ship with the crew, instead of being forced to attend the stuffy affairs of state. It still surprised her to this day that her father permitted her to remain onboard, under the careful watch of High Courtier Jaquobie. Oh, how he had tortured her during their etiquette lessons after that stunt.

A knock on the carriage window pulled her attention from the missive, her face breaking out into a smile as her eyes rested on the handsome, dark-haired figure. Lord Pettraud, the seventh son of Duke Pettraud, one of Saphire's greatest allies, trotted outside in the tropical sunlight atop his gallant horse. Always preferring to ride rather than sit in a carriage for endless hours, Perry gave her a comical wave pointing to some unseen sight ahead of their delegation. Rather than crane her neck to see what was coming, Jax watched her future consort thoughtfully. A mere day after her coronation to the Saphire throne, Perry had been presented as her future husband, an agreement Jax's father and Duke Pettraud had made unbeknownst to their children. Reluctant at first, Jax had negotiated a bit of a trial period for their courtship, feeling trapped by their looming engagement. To her delighted surprise, Perry quickly became one of her closest confidantes and friends, which blossomed into something deeper and more meaningful. While their engagement was not yet set in stone, it was all but inevitable. She had given her word to Duke Pettraud's courtiers that she would eventually wed Perry, yet she found herself longing for the day when

Perry himself would get down on one knee and formally ask for her hand.

"The Virtues be praised, Jax, look!" Uma lurched toward the window, her eyes widening in the direction where Perry had just pointed.

Shuffling her full skirts, Jax's amethyst eyes appraised the scene. As the carriage rolled over the peak of the hill, the port town of Tafreeni sprawled out before them. Narrow, spindle-like buildings clawed at the impossibly blue sky, the bright orange and green Tandora banners flying high in the wind. Through the towering structures, she caught a glimpse of sparkling water, the Sea of Intelligence caressing the shores of the realm.

When the Ancient Faith had been overthrown and the Virtues accepted as the official belief of the duchies, the oceans surrounding the continent had been renamed after the Four Virtues. In the north, the Brave Sea churned against the coastlines of Lysandeir and the Cetachi province. The Kind Sea shimmered along the southern duchies, while the Sea of Humility ran the length of the western nations. For the life of her, Jax could not pull the old names of the seas from her memory just now.

"Have you ever seen anything so stunning?" Uma said in awe, her eyes watering with emotion.

"Don't tell me that you think Tandora is more splendid than Saphire," Jax chided her lady's maid, trying to hide the teasing gleam in her gaze.

Uma paled and immediately clarified. "Of course not, Your Grace. Saphire is the ultimate gem in the Realm of Virtues." The poor young woman looked like she might cry at being misunderstood.

Jax broke into a fit of giggles. "Goodness, dear one, I was only joking! I know where your allegiance lies." She reached out and gave Uma's hand an affectionate squeeze. With the circumstances surrounding the Duchess's ascension to the throne, the two had grown incredibly close to one another, the line between servant and friend all but forgotten by Jax. "Just wait until you see the city from the water. It's quite breathtaking."

Uma fidgeted with the sleeve of her traveling clothes. "Are you sure this ship is safe enough for you to be on, Jax? I am a bit worried myself. And you won't even have the full Ducal Guard with you." Her chocolate brown eyes pleaded for assurance.

"I'll be perfectly safe," Jax promised. "Duke DeLacqua is sending a handful of his personal guardsmen to escort us on our journey to the island. *Rose of the Sea* is only carrying a handful of passengers. Captain Solomon will be all the protection we need."

As if on cue, the tanned face of the Captain of the Saphire Ducal Guard appeared in Uma's window. Noticing they were both staring at him, he gave the women an informal salute from atop his armored horse. George Solomon had joined the Ducal Guard at sixteen and quickly rose through the ranks, becoming the late Duke of Saphire's most trusted soldier. At thirty-six, he was the youngest man to hold the position, yet his kind brown eyes revealed he was an old soul. Growing up, Jax had a colossal crush on the man, with years of awkward encounters finally blossoming into true friendship. She was thankful he was accompanying her on this trip, despite his fear that the sea would not sit well with his stomach. As she watched him confidently bounce on his horse, she noticed that the Captain kept the medicinal pack Master Vyanti had given him tucked securely against his saddle. The guardsman was keen to protect the herbs that would ward off his seasickness. The royal physician had offered to pack the same plants for Jax, as well, but the sea did not trouble her.

"Have you met any of the others we will be traveling with?" Uma inquired, visibly nervous at the prospect of being around so many important people in such tight quarters.

Jax shook her head, frowning. "Interestingly enough, no. You'd think that the other duchies would at least send reputable proxies for Lady Carriena's birthday celebration, but I fear many of the dukedoms have scraped the bottom of the barrel for their emissaries."

"Not everyone is as fearless as you are," Uma said with a playful smile, although her eyes were still tinged with worry.

Jax waved a hand in a flippant gesture. "I'm sure the other passengers are using this voyage as leverage to elevate their standing back in their homelands. It will be surprising if the relationships we forge while on this little expedition are any help to Saphire at all." She leaned deeper into the cushion propped behind her slender frame. "Luckily, I don't really have to worry about expanding our influence. I am purely here to support and celebrate dear Carriena."

"High Courtier Jaquobie certainly wasn't impressed with your lack of preparation regarding the ship's manifest. I'm sure he would have loved to have known who you would be rubbing elbows with ahead of time," Uma said as she tried to suppress a scowl at the thought of the High Courtier.

"What our wonderful Jaquobie fails to realize is that I am considering this voyage a vacation. I simply refuse to be a Duchess until we arrive on Isla DeLacqua." Jax wrinkled her nose, then sighed.

Uma gave her a sad smile. "You can't turn off being a Duchess, Jax. It's not something you can escape."

For a moment, Jax remained silent, staring off into the distance. "I know. A girl can dream, right?" She met Uma's gaze with beseeching eyes. "It's just that it would be nice to not have the weight of the realm on my shoulders for a few days."

Uma answered with a sympathetic squeeze, her warm, calloused hand tightening over Jax's untarnished palm. They sat in companionable silence for a few moments before Uma sat up straight with excitement. "Why, the Virtues be praised."

Jax shifted to catch a glimpse of the sight, her own anticipation stirring in her stomach. Through the rambling towers and streets, impossibly blue water shimmered in the afternoon sun, inviting their caravan closer. As they rounded the final corner, arriving at the wharf, Jax laid her amethyst eyes on *Rose of the Sea.* The ship sat gracefully at the dock's edge, the water tossing it slightly side to side. Three strong, tall masts stretched into the cloudless sky, golden rope swinging from the myriad of rigging. The ship was a stunning creation. Jax clenched her hands with envy. Isla DeLacqua would be widely admired once word of the vessel's beauty traveled around the duchies.

The carriage rolled to a stop and the door swung open, held by an awestruck Hendrie, clearly absorbed in the ship's elegance rather than attending to the ladies inside the coach. Lord Pettraud's personal valet gawked several moments longer before shaking sense back into his head and snapping to attention. "Your Grace, we have arrived."

"I can see that," Jax said, smirking. She took Hendrie's extended hand as she climbed down from her seat. "What do you think of it?"

Hendrie blushed, embarrassed by her question. Jax knew she made the valet nervous, for the straw-haired, scrawny young man was not used to being in the presence of a Duchess. As Perry's valet, he often kept to himself, except when Perry needed his services or his companionship. When selecting who would make up the delegation for the trip, Hendrie made the cut because he was Perry's right-hand man, but Jax secretly hoped their close proximity would help alleviate Hendrie's acute bashfulness around her. She hated feeling that she intimidated those she considered to be friends.

"I never thought I'd ever be able to see anything so… so wondrous," Hendrie stuttered, finally able to put his words together. His brown eyes watered slightly. "Thank you for the chance, Duchess."

She gave his arm a squeeze before taking Perry's muscular arm, outstretched and waiting. "And what do you think, Lord Pettraud?"

Perry grinned at her slyly. "I think there is something much more beautiful in the harbor for me to appreciate than a ship." He wiggled an eyebrow, making her face flush at the suggestion.

Jax's flirtatious retort died on her lips as she spotted a flurry of movement from the ship's bow. "Carriena!" She failed at suppressing a squeal of glee as she recognized the figure dashing down the gangway.

Princess Carriena Lucia Brunovaris ran with abandon through the crowded wharf, disregarding all ceremony as she rushed up to Jax, flinging her arms around the Duchess. "I cannot believe you are here! I thought your letter of acceptance was too good to be true!"

Jax laughed, squeezing her friend so tightly they both struggled for breath. "How could I miss the chance to sail on the realm's most luxurious ship?" She giggled as Carriena pulled away from her. "Of course I am here to see you, dear one! It has been far too long." The sincerity in Jax's eyes expressed the honest truth.

Lady Carriena's short, stylishly-cropped blond hair blew in the wind, wisps of her bangs revealing lilac eyes, the sign of her ducal heritage. Jax was surprised to see a sadness behind the royal irises.

"What's wrong?"

Carriena took her in her arms once more. "I am so sorry you've been going through this all alone, Jax. I wish I could have been there to help." Her lips nearly touched Jax's burning ears as she whispered her regrets.

Jax held her Academy friend at an arm's length, giving her a reassuring smile. "Thank you, but I haven't been totally alone these past months. Lady Carriena, may I introduce you to Lord Pettraud, son of Duke Pettraud." Jax motioned to Perry, who had the sense to stand out of earshot while the women had their little reunion.

Carriena's eyes brightened with interest as she took in the handsome young lord. "I could hardly believe it when one of Father's courtiers told me the news. When is the wedding?"

Perry's face turned beet red as he sputtered, and Jax, too, felt as if she'd been put on the spot. "Well, truth be told, our engagement has not been made official yet, but we intend to move forward, soon." Jax cast Perry a pleading look for support, but his eyes were firmly planted on the ground in embarrassment.

The devilish gleam in Carriena's eyes told Jax her friend was purposefully fueling the flame. "Not official? My, Lord Pettraud, what are you waiting for?" she said in jest.

Jax elbowed Carriena hard in the ribs, her friend nearly doubling over in both pain and laughter.

"All right, all right. I've had my fun. Lord Pettraud, it is an honor to have you aboard *Rose of the Sea* for her maiden voyage." Carriena's giggling subsided, and her face returned to an uncharacteristically formal expression. "If you will both excuse me for just a moment, I must let my other guests know that we will be setting sail now that you've arrived. Captain Valhalen will escort you on board and show you to your staterooms." Carriena raised her hand, signaling to a tall figure limping down the causeway. "We shall catch up once everyone is settled on board, Jax," she said as she leaned in to peck her friend on the cheek. With a twirl of her blue and white traveling gown, she disappeared back into the crowd.

"Have you recovered?" Jax asked Perry, whose face had finally lost its red hue. "I told you, she can be a bit of a windstorm."

"You call that a windstorm? That woman is a bloody hurricane."

Perry chuckled, taking the ribbing Lady Carriena had given him in good stride. Jax knew her friend had only been teasing him, but she also wished he'd taken the hint.

"Duchess Saphire, I presume?" A gravelly voice interrupted them, pulling their attention to a white-uniformed man with a dark black beard streaked with white. His face was weathered and pink, with blisters from the sun's reflection sprouting across his ruddy cheeks. "I am Viktor Valhalen, Captain of *Rose of the Sea*." He bowed at the waist in a courteous, yet stiff gesture.

"Yes, I am Duchess Saphire, but you are free to address me by my given name. I prefer Jacqueline to Saphire. It makes me feel like more of a person than a figurehead." Jax extended her hand and Valhalen took it reverently for a kiss.

"Duchess Jacqueline, then. Forgive me, Your Grace. I am not accustomed to interacting with such esteemed company," he said, appearing uncomfortable in her presence.

She went to work putting him at ease. "Nothing to forgive, Captain. Congratulations on your appointment. You must be thrilled to command the realm's most glorious ship." Her eyes traveled up the tallest of the three masts, the sight impressing her once more.

Valhalen shifted from one foot to the other. "It is the greatest honor a man of the sea such as myself could ever have. I am indebted to Duke DeLacqua for his kindness."

George Solomon appeared from behind the carriage, saluting the sea captain and introducing himself. "I understand your crew has also been appointed by the Duke of Isla DeLacqua. Have you sailed with any of the men before?"

Valhalen snorted. "Only my first mate, my eldest son. The others on board came highly recommended by the Duke and had excellent references from their previous employers. I'm not one to put my life in someone else's hands, but I trust these men enough. The ship doesn't require many hands; the Tandorians designed her to travel light and fast, with more room for guests than staff. Seventeen men make up my crew, along with eight of DeLacqua's Ducal Guard, two cooks, and three pursers. I suspect you'll want to see their logs?"

George nodded firmly. "Yes, for the Duchess's safety, I will want to meet and review the crew before we leave port."

The Captain sighed at the security measures. "Well, let me take you on board so we can get this over and done with. I'd like to set sail as soon as possible."

"Captain Solomon, if Duke DeLacqua has already taken the proper measures to assemble this crew, perhaps we can trust his judgement?" Jax suggested, not wanting to make a fuss and hold up the voyage any longer than their late arrival apparently had.

"I respectfully disagree, Your Grace," George answered curtly, his dark eyes telling her that he would not budge. "Your safety is of the utmost importance, and it would be negligent to not interview these men myself."

Choosing her battles, she nodded in acceptance. She knew George well enough to know he would not back down when it came to her protection. "Very well, Captain, we shall see you on deck."

Valhalen motioned to the crowded dock, a young man pushing his way through the throngs of people. "This is my son, Jogan. He will personally assist your valet with your belongings and show you to your staterooms aboard."

Jogan smiled at the group, his freckled face and wide brown eyes immediately putting Jax at ease. After a clumsy bow, the young man helped Hendrie with the trunks, leading the way down the wharf.

As they drew closer to the ship, Jax was once again astounded by the sheer size of the craft, wondering how it managed to stay afloat. The golden ropes twinkled in the sun, casting swirling shadows against the polished wooden planks. The carpeted gangway was soft under her feet, breathlessly transporting her on board the regal vessel. Up close, *Rose of the Sea* was even more opulent than it appeared from the docks. Silver and gold were laid into nearly every surface Jax could see. Even the buckets for washing the decks were trimmed with precious metals.

"This way, Your Grace. Lady Carriena has you in the Diamond Suite. Lord Pettraud, you will be in the Emerald Suite," Jogan huffed as he hoisted Jax's heavy trunk up a steep staircase that led to the upper level of the deck. "The Diamond, Rose, and Emerald Suites are near the Captain's Cabin on the upper deck. Beautiful views. The rest of our guests will be below you on the lower deck in their own private rooms."

"I'm sure that will be a rude awakening for some of them," Perry whispered dryly. Jax responded by shooting a look of daggers his way.

"Each suite has a side room for your servants, as well, so they will never be far away from you if you require their assistance," Jogan explained as he arrived at the first door in the long corridor, green jewels sparkling from the firelight twinkling from wall sconces.

While Jax was relieved Uma would be near, she regretted the first mate's curt words. Uma was more than a servant she had at her beck and call. She was her friend. "And where will Captain Solomon be sleeping? I think my guardsman should be stationed near me."

Jogan's face registered her words blankly, the young officer quickly becoming flustered. "Well, I'm not entirely sure, Your Grace." Placing Jax's trunk on the floor with an awkward thud, he fumbled for a piece of parchment in his back pocket. "We don't have him listed on the ship's manifest for some reason," Jogan croaked, swallowing his embarrassment. "I was under the impression that Duke DeLacqua had sent a handful of guards to watch over his daughter and guests. We weren't expecting any other officers, unfortunately."

Annoyed, Jax opened her mouth, but Perry's cheery voice cut her off. "Captain Solomon can share my suite. I'm sure you have an extra bedroll on board?" He looked at the first mate expectantly, who answered with a furious nod. "There, that's settled. It looks like my room is just down the hall from yours, Your Grace, so Captain Solomon won't be far away."

Jax rolled her eyes at Perry's skillful problem solving. "So it would seem, Lord Pettraud." She watched Hendrie shuffle through the emerald-gilded door with Perry's trunk, her eyes trailing further down the passage. "Enjoy your bunkmate." She gave him a teasing smile before following Jogan to a diamond-studded door that she could only assume was the entrance to her suite.

"Please join Lady Carriena and the rest of her guests up on the top deck as soon as you've settled in, Your Grace. My father hopes to be underway within the hour, and there will be a sunset cocktail party to celebrate." Jogan grunted as he placed Jax's trunk at the foot of the enormous canopy bed that sat pristinely in the middle of her room, bowing as he departed, leaving the Duchess and Uma to fawn over the elaborate quarters.

Jax found it hard to believe she was still standing on a boat. The suite looked more beautiful than many of the apartments she had stayed in over the years while visiting various castles around the realm. The Tandorian artists who'd crafted this vessel really had outdone themselves. "Well, Uma, I must say, I was not expecting this level of luxury," she murmured with appreciation.

Uma nodded beside her. "Indeed. I'm glad I packed some of your finer gowns for the journey, or these silk sheets would have put you to shame." She snapped open Jax's large trunk, assessing the wardrobe inside. "We haven't left port yet, Your Grace. There's still time to back out of this. Are you sure you will be safe enough on board with so few guardsmen?"

The Duchess gave her friend a severe stare. "I appreciate the concern, dear one, but let's put this matter to rest once and for all. I trust Lady Carriena with my life, and I trust Duke DeLacqua as much as I trust Duke Pettraud or Mensina. George will be protection enough, especially with our suites tucked away from everyone else on board." Jax wandered over to her trunk to stroke a beautiful, shimmering blue evening gown. "Now, let's get ready for some fun."

Chapter Two

Jax felt the ship lurch forward under her chair with startling force. Uma stumbled in surprise, leaving a trail of rouge on the Duchess's face as a result. "For Virtue's sake," Uma grumbled, setting to work on wiping away the excess red blush. "Are these the kind of working conditions I should expect going forward?"

Jax chuckled at her lady's maid's frustration. "I look good enough for now, my dear. No one will be looking at my face once they see the sunset dancing across these sparkling waters. Come on, let us go up to the top deck and have a look at the harbor," she breathlessly teased, rushing toward the door of her suite. As much as she wanted Uma to experience the beauty of the open seas, Jax, too, was excited to witness the humbling sight. Hurrying down the long corridor in her ocean blue gown, she knocked on Perry's door, with no response. He and Hendrie must already be at the cocktail hour Carriena was hosting.

"Your Grace? May I help you?" Jogan's friendly voice floated down the passage from the doorway of what must be the Captain's Cabin.

Jax smiled, curiously glancing behind the young man as he shut the large door with a snap. "Uma and I were just heading upstairs to meet everyone."

Jogan nodded in acknowledgement. "I shall accompany you

back up. I was just grabbing some star charts for my father. Our guests from Zaltor were interested in viewing them." He motioned to three large rolls of aged parchment tucked under his arm.

"Is that what a first mate does? Fetches papers for the ship's captain?" Uma's forehead wrinkled in confusion, clearly uncertain of Jogan's role aboard *Rose of the Sea.*

If he took offense to her question, Jogan disguised it, merely laughing it off. "I suppose the line between first mate and son is quite blurry for my father. But I take it in stride. I know I'm the only one he trusts in this part of the ship, regardless of his confidence in the crew Duke DeLacqua commissioned. The rotating Ducal Guards stationed at the doors leading out to the main decks are not allowed to let anyone but my father, Lady Carriena, of course our friends from Saphire, and myself through the doors…under penalty of death."

Jax could tell from the first mate's tone that he was trying to put them at ease, reassuring her and Uma that they were well protected and safe from anyone else on board, even the other crew members. "I'm heartened to know your father takes his position so seriously, Jogan. I will make sure to pass my compliments to Duke DeLacqua once we make it safely across the sea." She paused for only a moment. "Now, will you escort Uma and myself up to the festivities? I am eager to meet our other traveling companions. You say there's a group from Zaltor?"

Nodding enthusiastically, Jogan extended his free arm to the Duchess and led them through the double doors at the end of the hall, the salty sea air whipping across Jax's cheeks. From over the railings on the lower deck, she could see the harbor shimmering in the late afternoon sun, purples and pinks slinking across the tops of rolling waves. The spiral-domed buildings of Tafreeni stretched up into the sky, signaling their stoic goodbyes.

"What a sight," Uma marveled in fascination from beside her sovereign.

Jax looked at Uma's awestruck face and squeezed her hand with tenderness. "I agree, my dear, but I must ask you keep your admiration in check as we meet the other guests. I don't need anyone seeing your desire to move to Tandora and using it against me." While Jax mainly meant for her words to be taken in jest, they nevertheless held an air of truth. Even though she was vacationing, she was still Duchess of Saphire, the most powerful duchy in the Realm of Virtues. She was not naïve enough to expect a vacation from politics.

"Everyone is gathering on the top deck, Your Grace," Jogan instructed, directing Jax and Uma up an elegant set of stairs to their right. "If you'll excuse me, I must get these to my father." With that, Jogan hopped off the steps and strutted over toward the lone door on the quarter deck.

"Shall we?" Jax said with a wink, following Jogan's directions up the red carpeted staircase. Unlike most ships she'd seen in her day, the sheer size of *Rose of the Sea*'s top deck astounded her. It was nearly the width of a small banquet hall, and just as long. Its size was made all the more apparent by the gathered crowd taking up only a fraction of the space.

In the middle of the group, Lady Carriena's blond hair glistened in the dusk, her giggles bubbling up to fill the soaring sails overhead. "And here she is now, ladies and gentlemen! My dearest friend from the Academy, Duchess Jacqueline Arienta Xavier of Saphire." Racing to Jax's side, Carriena hugged her tightly, breaking all the rules of etiquette without regret. Jax normally would not have minded the display of affection, but she was now amongst strangers, and she needed to assert her power.

"Saphire is delighted to partake in this maiden voyage," Jax said, formidably turning to the assembled crowd. "We always enjoy visiting the smaller nations of the realm." She flashed her amethyst eyes quickly to meet Carriena's amused smirk, begging her friend for forgiveness for the political slight.

If she took offense to the remark, Carriena waved it aside. "I must introduce you, Duchess, to the rest of my father's guests, and then we shall retire to the dining hall for a feast fit for a ducal table." Holding out a slender arm, Lady Carriena encouraged the first couple forward. "May I introduce Charles and Giovanna, brother and sister of House Montivarius."

Jax's eyes lit up in recognition as she heard the name. "It is a pleasure to meet you both. Are you any relation to the Hestian playwright, Michelangelo Montivarius?"

Tall and lanky, Sir Charles stepped forward and bowed, his shaggy blond hair falling into his amber eyes. "Indeed, Your Grace. He is our father."

Lady Giovanna, who appeared to be a few years younger than her brother, curtsied, her small frame trembling with the anticipation of meeting the famed sovereign. "Are you familiar with his work, Duchess?" Her eyes were the same amber color as her brother's, marking their noble heritage.

"The last time I was in Hestes, I attended the opening night of *A Glass Thorn*. Simply stunning," Jax said, smiling at the memory.

"My sister made her debut in that play," Charles gushed with pride as Giovanna's cheeks reddened with embarrassment.

Jax looked at the ashen-haired woman once more, trying to place her. "Oh, I remember! You played the merchant's daughter. Your voice was quite lovely."

"I am hoping I can convince Lady Giovanna to perform for us as we sail to Isla DeLacqua," Carriena said, giving the young actress a coaxing grin. Without waiting for a reply from either Montivarius sibling, she turned to the next awaiting guests. "Duchess, this is Lady Florence and Sir Ernest of House Haulsinger from Savant."

Before Jax could properly react, a bulbous, impossibly old man waddled forward and took her hand in his own, placing a slobbering kiss on her fingers. His tiny eyes roamed languidly up her slender figure, finally letting go of her hand and stepping back. "Duquessa, it is an honor to be in your presence. My wife and I have heard nothing but fine things about you and your duchy." His wiry gray hair whipped wildly in the wind, revealing a large bald spot on the very top of his oversized head.

Jax controlled her laughter at the man's chaotic appearance, turning to his wife in greeting, surprised that she was the exact opposite of her husband. Elegant and refined, despite her rather plain wardrobe, Lady Florence curtsied with stiffness, her willowy figure barely moving, signaling her advanced age. "It is a pleasure to meet you, Duquessa."

In a whirlwind, Carriena moved on to a strapping middle-aged man with dark hair and bright, almost orange eyes. "This is Sir Archer of House Orchid from Tandora. He is the master builder who designed *Rose of the Sea.*"

Jax gasped with delight. "I had no idea we would be traveling with the artist behind this beautiful specimen. I hope you won't object if I try to solicit a ship of my own for Saphire." Her eyes crinkled with mischief.

Master Archer laughed, a hearty sound that raked through the air. "No rest for the weary, I suppose. It would be an honor to be commissioned to create such a piece for you, Your Grace."

"Jacqueline, we're not even out of the harbor and you're already trying to best me," Carriena chided, her joke sizzling between the two friends. "Let Master Archer rest one day before you try to outdo me, all right?" Not waiting for Jax's playful retort, she brought forward the last three guests. "May I introduce Vincent and Hazel Quorimander of Zaltor, and Monsieur Grandeair of Crepsta."

It had been years since Jax had ventured to the deserts of Zaltor or interacted with any of its nobility. Appraising the couple, Jax was taken in by their exquisite beauty, their dark skin emphasizing the heated yellow flecks in their amber eyes. Hazel's black hair was piled regally on her head, her slender neck dripping with red gems native to the region. Vincent, too, was adorned in fine jewelry, his short cropped dark hair revealing gold hoops hanging from his ears.

Monsieur Grandeair, on the other hand, was a nondescript gentleman whose tunic appeared to be a bit too tight for his barrel chest. His pale skin seemed to be infused with an olive tinge, his forehead sweating profusely. "Are you feeling under the weather, Monsieur?" Jax inquired with concern.

The older man coughed. "Just a bit, Your Grace. It seems my sea legs are still dawdling about on land."

Lady Carriena frowned. "I had hoped the fresh air up on deck might do the monsieur some good, but it appears not."

Hazel stepped forward, her jewel-laden hand outstretched. "Perhaps if he tried a bit of gingerroot, his health might improve," she purred as she placed what appeared to be a tiny plant stem in the man's clammy hand.

Jax looked at her inquisitively, wondering where the woman's knowledge of herbal remedies came from. As if sensing the question, Hazel spoke. "In Zaltor, I am a High Priestess of the Ancient Faith,

Your Grace. At an early age, we are trained in nature's powers."

Jax struggled to keep her face neutral. The Ancient Faith was an archaic religion with a tumultuous history. While Saphire, under her father's command, protected its believers, the Ancient Faith always made Jax uncomfortable. She had been brought up to believe in kindness, bravery, intelligence, and humility, not demons and gods who supposedly dictated the lives of men.

"I can see by your face that you are not a believer, yet Saphire is one of the foremost duchies promoting tolerance of the Ancient Faith," Vincent said. "You do not shun what you do not understand. That, I think, is a good virtue." His soft, silky voice drew her attention to the attractive nobleman. His words were kind and full of praise.

"My father often said that just because something didn't make sense to me, didn't mean it wasn't good in its own right," Jax recalled, her father's handsome face filling her memories.

"Vyanti is right to serve by your side, Duchess," Hazel said, her hypnotic gaze watching Jax's surprise.

"You know Master Vyanti?" Jax hadn't realized her royal physician had traveled to Zaltor.

"I spent some of my youth in Saphire, specifically to train with the revered priest. The Faith was shocked when he announced he would serve as royal physician to a Virtuous duke," Hazel explained, her eyes examining every inch of Jax's face for her reaction.

"I am extremely grateful he did. Master Vyanti is a great friend and mentor," Jax replied, putting to bed the topic of the Ancient Faith. Even though she promoted tolerance amongst her people, she had a tough time shaking the uncomfortable notion that gods were watching over them. She turned her attention back to Monsieur Grandeair, who was crunching away on the gingerroot, a rosy pink returning to his cheeks. "Has the High Priestess saved the day, Monsieur?"

The stout man nodded furiously, his warm, caramel eyes filling with gratitude. "I believe so. Virtues praise you, Lady Hazel."

Jax rolled her eyes at the man's obliviousness to her beliefs, which she quickly realized Hazel caught. The two women shared a secret smile before their focus was captured by their hostess.

"Now that we have all been introduced, let us proceed to the dining hall for a little celebratory feast," Lady Carriena squealed with eagerness, taking Jax by the arm and guiding her down another set of carpeted stairs to the main deck. In the shadow of a stairwell leading up to the bow, an ornately carved door swung open invitingly. As Carriena and Jax approached, an illuminated foyer sprawled out before them in the belly of the ship. "The set of stairs in the corner leads down to the galley and the service quarters. Ahead are the dining room and ballroom."

"You've got a ballroom on this thing, have you?" Jax almost choked at the absurdity, her friend tittering beside her.

"Well, I hardly think it's big enough to spin around in, but Father insists we call it a ballroom. Makes our guests drool with envy," Carriena said as she mimed wiping the corner of Jax's mouth.

Jax batted her hands away. "Quite the guest list you've assembled. How did this mismatched group come to be?"

Carriena's expression turned sour. "If I'd had my way, just you and I would be sailing across the sea, but no, my birthday also has to double as a political play for more power." She bit her lip and lowered her voice, obviously not wishing to be overheard as they walked into the cavernous dining room. "I probably shouldn't be telling you this, but I'm so perturbed with Father that I don't care. He's in the middle of renegotiating Isla DeLacqua's wine and mead suppliers with a few vineyards in Hestes. House Montivarius is in good standing with our favored vendor, but Father wants a fairer price. He thinks that if he can woo the Montivarius siblings, they'll put in a good word for us and get our costs lowered." She paused to glance around and make sure no one stood within earshot. "We're spending so much money having goods ferried over to the island, I think Father is growing concerned about our treasury. That's why Monsieur Grandeair is aboard. He ran a successful bank of some sort back in Crepsta, and my father has asked him to review Isla DeLacqua's finances. Rather boring, if you ask me. We're also having a bit of trouble with a few clans that preach the Ancient Faith. I think he's hoping that having a High Priestess as a guest will soothe the tension."

"And what about your friends from Savant?" Jax found it incredulous that her friend could divulge such highly sensitive information without a second thought.

"Oh goodness, the Haulsingers. They are a favored house by Duke Savant. Father wants a lesser tax on cloth imports, and thinks the Haulsingers can convince the Duke to make it happen. Although I wouldn't be surprised if they both keel over and die; they both are so decrepitly old." Carriena sighed with a dramatic flair, giving Jax a bored look.

While it saddened the Duchess that her friend felt like her birthday was being turned into a political spectacle, she couldn't help but feel disappointed by Carriena's lack of propriety. Carriena would assume the throne once her father either stepped down or passed away, and dealings like these were like breathing air to a strong ruler. "Well, it's all good practice for when the crown is resting on your head, my dear," Jax said, gently reminding Carriena that she did not have the luxury of having a normal birthday like most people. "At least all this is going to play out on this gorgeous vessel."

"If I survive it," Carriena mumbled, almost so inaudibly that Jax wondered if she'd misheard.

By now, the guests had filtered into the lavish dining hall, everyone in awe of the dazzling chandelier flickering overhead. A long mahogany table stretched out across the room, big enough for nearly thirty guests. Someone had laid out golden place settings at the end of the table closest to the entrance they'd just arrived through. Jax caught sight of two men clad in smart-looking black uniforms waiting by a table in the shadows, ready to pour honeyed mead for the guests. As much as she wanted to grab an entire bottle for herself, Jax managed to keep her hands at her sides as she made her way to her seat.

As hostess, Lady Carriena took the throne-like chair at the head of the table, motioning for Jax to sit beside her. "Ah, Lord Pettraud, please take the seat to my left. I must learn all about the man who intends to *someday* marry my dearest friend." Carriena's words caused a flurry of dubious looks to be exchanged around the table, each guest taking a seat where dictated. With Perry directly across from her, Jax's dining companion to her left was Ernest Haulsinger with Charles Montivarius sitting beside Perry. Scanning the length of the table, Jax was relieved to see that Captain Solomon, Hendrie, and

Uma were all seated together, graciously included in the evening's festivities.

"Before we begin," Lady Carriena announced, "I just wanted to once again welcome you all on the maiden voyage of my beloved *Rose of the Sea*. May the Virtues fill our sails and see us safely home!" She raised a brimming gold goblet into the air in reverence, everyone else following suit. "Cheers, and enjoy tonight's meal, prepared by our renowned resident chef, Monsieur Devoyier."

At her cue, the doors at the back of the dining hall swung open, and the two men Jax had seen in the shadows earlier rolled two enormous trays of covered platters out into the light. The smell of roasted duck and chicken reached her nose before a steaming dish was placed in front of her. Her mouth watered; she hadn't eaten anything since a light picnic lunch back in the carriage, and her stomach raged in protest. As she tucked into her meal, she kept a mindful eye on the dessert display on a nearby table. She would need to save room for that brambleberry tart.

"Are you a patron of the theater, Lord Pettraud?" Charles Montivarius asked conversationally, just as Perry took in a large mouthful of glazed duck.

Nodding as he haphazardly chewed, Perry wiped away remnants of the colossal bite. "Indeed. My mother and I frequented the theater in Pettraud's capital quite often before she passed." He pierced another piece of meat with vigor. "It appears I was the only one out of my brothers who knew how much it meant to her. It was one of her favorite things to do." Seeing his eyes go a bit glassy, Jax was surprised by Perry's willingness to speak about his beloved late mother. It took her only a moment to realize that his goblet of mead was already empty. His cheeks flushed when he met her bemused gaze. "Why, I believe one of the last shows we saw together was one by your father, Sir Charles." Perry turned his attention back toward the impressed young man.

"Are you involved with the productions, as well?" Jax took the reins of the conversation, somewhat nervous that Perry's judgment might be skewed by the spirits he so freely drank.

Charles shook his head, his blond hair swaying across his eyes. "I took a different path than my sister, actually. I'm currently studying to be a physician at the Academy."

Jax's eyes lit up at the mention of her alma mater. "I remember how rigorous the curriculum was said to be for aspiring healers. Is Master Jololian still teaching?"

Clearly pleased that he had found common ground with the Duchess, Charles grinned. "The nasty ol' bugger is still requiring three parchments a night."

Jax chuckled with grace, remembering the countless times she, Carriena, and her childhood friend Aranelda were scolded by the ancient professor for making too much noise in the hallways. The memory of the three friends together threatened to tear a hole in her heart after what had happened between her and Arnie. "How did you ever manage to secure time away from your studies for this voyage?"

At this, Charles suddenly grew somber. "I'm afraid I won't be making the roundtrip journey. I will be staying on in Isla DeLacqua to apprentice with the Duke's court physician."

"Master Kah is one of the most skilled healers throughout the realm. My father brought him on as court physician nearly fifteen years ago from Zaltor," Carriena said with pride, motioning toward where Hazel sat, her posture perfect. "I believe he is the High Priestess's uncle."

Jax peered over at the stoic woman, her expression curious. Hazel had not mentioned she had relatives in Isla DeLacqua. She knew the Duke's reason for inviting Hazel was to settle the hostility growing among the Ancient Faith. Perhaps the High Priestess had accepted the invitation for the chance at a family reunion. "How long will you be studying at Master Kah's side, Sir Charles?" Jax asked, turning her attention back to the young man.

He sighed, looking tired. "For as long as he sees fit."

Ernest Haulsinger looked up from his meal, fidgeting beside Jax. "Seems like a long road of uncertainty is ahead of you, my boy," the old man barked, bits of chicken and greens spewing onto the place setting before him.

His nose wrinkling in disgust at the man's lack of manners, Charles merely nodded.

"Do you travel often, Sir Ernest?" Perry quipped, making light of the old man's behavior.

"I try not to, but Florence practically dragged me out of bed for this trip. I'm much more content sitting in my parlor, watching the world outside my window. This sea travel is much too boisterous for my old bones," Ernest huffed before shoveling whipped potatoes into his gaping mouth.

"Sir Ernest has always enjoyed the comforts of home." Carriena smiled through the man's unpleasantries. "His wife, Lady Florence, was once one of the most gifted clothing designers in all of Savant. She's traveled to every duchy over the course of her career, I believe."

"Is your wife retired now, Sir Ernest?" Perry inquired.

The man's jowls swung lazily as he shook his head. "She still dabbles in the occasional design here and there, but her hands are beginning to get the better of her." To emphasize his wife's predicament, he reared a gnarled hand of his own in the air. "The new, younger tailors are taking over the scene, as they call it, in Savant."

Jax glanced down the table, noting that while Lady Florence was listening to an animated Master Archer, her amber eyes were distant and laced with sadness. Jax couldn't imagine the heartache one must suffer when they can no longer partake in their passion. "I would love to see her designs at some point."

"I'm sure she'd happily show you," Ernest grumbled. "She brought a sample to show Duke DeLacqua. She seems to think that she still has a chance at becoming a royal tailor. At her age, I keep telling her to give it up. Silly woman."

Jax raised her eyebrows unabashedly, offended by this man's lack of decency, especially toward his wife. Lady Carriena, too, placed her napkin down on the table and sent him a stern look. "I have had the good fortune to see Lady Florence's designs, and she is truly gifted. I'm sure my father will come to some arrangement with your wife regarding her skills."

Ernest merely batted the terse statement away, resuming his battle with a meaty chicken leg.

Jax and Carriena shared an eye roll. Although clearly unpleasant, Sir Ernest Haulsinger had just revealed what his wife truly wanted more than anything else. Jax could see the gears turning behind Carriena's light lilac eyes. She, too, understood that Duke DeLacqua could bestow a ceremonial position to Lady Florence as royal tailor in exchange for using her influence with Duke Savant to lower the cloth tax. A wink told Jax that Carriena would be laying the groundwork throughout the rest of the journey.

†

"Quite a successful start *Rose of the Sea* is off to, no?" Carriena said with amusement later on during the meal, popping a chocolate-covered strawberry into her delicate mouth.

Finishing off the last bite of the brambleberry tart, Jax closed her eyes, savoring the flavor. "What, the fact that we haven't sunk yet?"

Carriena swatted her arm playfully, tutting under her breath. "Hush now. I don't want any negative thoughts to even remotely curse us."

"I can assure you, Lady Carriena, that *Rose of the Sea* is nearly indestructible. I'd like to see a wave that could smash this Tandorian hull," boasted Archer, the master builder, throwing back another swig of mead.

"Well, I wouldn't like to see that at all," Monsieur Grandeair snapped, his face once again laced with seasickness. He took out a handkerchief and wiped the beads of sweat from his balding head, his nerves clearly getting the better of him.

"Shall I fetch you some more gingerroot, perhaps, Monsieur?" Hazel offered, her regal voice like velvet in the dying dining chatter.

"I have some smelling salts that might be of assistance," Charles offered, clearly eager to showcase his talents as a physician-in-training.

"I'm fine, I'm fine," Monsieur Grandeair reassured them all, folding his damp handkerchief with care. Jax's keen eyes noticed that the cloth was embroidered artistically with golden thread.

"That's a beautiful piece, Monsieur," she commented, enchanted by the intricately woven designs. She couldn't imagine ever using something so lovely to wipe away sweat.

Grandeair glanced at her before looking appraisingly at the cloth. Frowning, he tucked it away. "Picked this up from a Cetachi merchant. It's one of a kind, very rare."

Beside her, Ernest grunted to life. "And I'm sure very expensive. Those Cetachi rebels are always bleeding people dry."

Monsieur Grandeair managed a bleak chuckle. "Well, I know something about bleeding people dry, too." He looked around the room, but was met with blank, confused stares. "While by profession, I am a banker, my fortune has been made over the years in private loans. Why, I have financed nearly half the merchants and craftsmen in Crepsta, and even some in other duchies. It's a tricky business when people cannot pay on their debts, but I never meet my clients face-to-face. I hire other people to do the nasty parts." He gazed at each guest for confirmation, leaving everyone to shift uncomfortably in their seats.

Jax snuck a look at Carriena, wondering if the Duke knew about Monsieur Grandeair's side dealings. While her face revealed nothing, Jax saw a spark twinkling behind her eyes. Obviously, the Duchy of DeLacqua wanted to make use of all Monsieur Grandeair's monetary talents.

Carriena cleared her throat, pulling the attention of the room to her. "I realize that we all have had a long day of travel. Might I suggest a quick nightcap in the ballroom before we retire for the evening?" She motioned down the table. "Perhaps Lady Giovanna would regale us with a song?"

Clearly not expecting to be put on the spot, Lady Giovanna's face glowed with a combination of embarrassment and too much mead. "Your Highness, I'm not sure I'm in the right frame of mind to give you the performance you deserve."

"Nonsense! I'm sure you will sound lovely. Besides, we've all had as much to drink as you have, my dear, so it's doubtful we'll even notice a difference." Carriena's dismissive cackled made Jax suddenly fretful that her friend had indeed indulged too much.

Not wanting the future Duchess of Isla DeLacqua to do something she would regret in the morning, Jax stood up from the table with as much stately sophistication as she could muster, the alcohol affecting her just enough to leave her feeling off balance. "I believe Lady Carriena is right in that we all have had our fair share of honeyed mead, and it would be tragic for Lady Giovanna's talents to be wasted on muted ears. I suggest we all say goodnight and leave the merriment for tomorrow. Come, Lady Carriena, I shall escort you to your chambers." Giving Perry a slight nod to head for the door, Jax grabbed their hostess more forcefully than the young woman was probably expecting, propelling her out of the room and into the salty sea air.

"What was that about? The night is young, let's have ourselves some fun," Carriena said with a childish pout as Jax and Perry escorted her toward the upper cabin deck, Captain Solomon, Hendrie, and Uma obediently following.

"My darling friend, you still cannot hold your liquor," Jax hissed, thinking back to the few times the two had raided a professor's brandy chest for a forbidden drink. "We're not at the Academy anymore, Carriena. While I know you wanted this to be a fun celebration of your birthday, you must remember we are on a ship in the middle of the sea, surrounded by political players we know very little about. We must keep our wits about us."

Carriena hung her head, the air sobering her into shame. "You make it sound as though we need to be worried about something, Jax."

"I don't mean to sound reprimanding, but you should be worried." Jax softened her tone. "You need to make sure these guests see you as someone to be revered if you want to have any hope in making these deals your father has been negotiating stick. You cannot let your guard down, dearest, not even for a moment. It would be unwise." She placed a comforting hand on Carriena's arm.

"Sounds like an awful way to live," Carriena murmured, her shoulders slumping in defeat.

Jax gave her a sad smile. "You get used to it. It's a small price to pay in order to make a difference in the lives of your people. People who trust and depend on you to keep them safe."

"They depend on my father. I'm just the flighty princess who keeps them entertained with her missteps." Bitterness laced Carriena's words.

"I thought the very same thing about myself. But now, I am the one Saphire depends on. Someday, you will bear the mantle of DeLacqua. You cannot escape your birthright," Jax responded in a firm, but caring tone.

Staring up into the midnight sky, Carriena stood silent for a long moment. Finally, she closed her eyes and took a deep breath, nodding. "You're right, Jax. I'm only kidding myself to think I can escape the inevitable. It just seems so impossible. Me, a Duchess. How did you come to terms with it?"

Jax pulled her beautiful friend aside, out of earshot of her Saphirian companions. "Truth be told, I am still coming to terms with it. But may the Virtues strike me down if I ever let anyone see that kind of weakness. Because we cannot afford to be weak, Carriena. We must be strong. Strong for our people, strong for our duchies, and strong for ourselves. I know you have that strength inside of you." She folded her arms around the young woman and gave her a reassuring squeeze. "Now, let's get you inside. You'll freeze to death in that gorgeous dress of yours."

Joining the others, Jax and Carriena led the way up to the staterooms, the entrance manned by a new pair of guards, who nodded in greeting as they opened the door to the cabin passageway. Uma took Carriena's arm and led her down to the Rose Suite. "I'll help her prepare for bed, Your Grace, then come see to you."

Jax reached out and fondly touched Uma's cheek. "Thank you, Uma. Take your time."

Perry, George, and Hendrie all waited until Carriena was safely in her room with the door shut before turning their eyes to Jax. "Everything all right?" Perry asked, clearly bemused by the night's events.

"I think so. I hope Carriena's behavior hasn't damaged her favor with any of the other guests." Jax cast a worried glance to each of the three men before her.

"Your presence by her side is definitely reassuring, Your Grace," George formally reported. "At least, Lady Florence and Master Archer seemed to think your influence was needed to steer the evening in the right direction." George had been sitting close to Archer and Lady Florence throughout the dinner.

"Yes, and Lady Giovanna was certainly relieved you interceded on her behalf. She's not a woman of many words, but her expression conveyed her gratitude that she did not have to perform tonight,"

Hendrie recounted.

"What an odd group of people we are traveling with," Jax mused, looking down the deserted passage, wondering how the rest of the guests were settling into their cabins on the level below them.

"I'm sure they'll keep us entertained for the remainder of the voyage," Perry said with a chuckle, although Jax noticed a hint of uneasiness brewing behind his lavender eyes.

Perhaps it was the honeyed mead going to her head, but the more she thought about the scene at dinner, something told her that this group of passengers was going to be more than Jax bargained for.

Chapter Three

The pale peach sky took Jax's breath away, the sun winking into existence in the east, casting shimmering rays across the infinitely blue water. Loose strands of her caramel hair whipped across her face, the salty wind billowing in her linen skirts. The crisp smell cleared her head, foggy shadows of the night before seeping into memory. As she looked out across the seemingly endless waters, she pledged to avoid any more mead on this trip; she needed to be clearheaded in order to properly watch over her friend.

"A beautiful vision to behold so early in the morning." Perry's voice drifted up onto the deck of the bow, his unruly dark hair appearing at the top of the stairs.

"Yes, you certainly don't wake up to a sight like this in Saphire," Jax murmured in agreement, giving him a smile.

"I meant you, Duchess." He arrived at her side and placed a tender kiss on her blushing cheek. His bright eyes meandered down the length of her simple, pale blue frock before settling back on her face with a dashing smile. "Up early?"

Winded for only a moment under the intensity of his stare, Jax nodded. "I wanted to see the sun rise before the chaos of the day begins."

"Chaos?" Perry leaned against the railing of the ship, scanning the expansive sea before them.

"You might think me paranoid, but I had a hard time shaking the unsettling feeling I had last night. I didn't sleep very well. I spent the whole time thinking about our dinner guests," Jax admitted in a quiet tone.

"What about them? Truth be told, besides the Master Builder, we're traveling with a relatively unremarkable group of people," Perry said in a flippant manner.

"I thought that I was the only sovereign in attendance because no one else of my station wanted to risk the journey," Jax said with a childish scowl. "But it turns out I was the only one invited, and it seems only because I am Carriena's oldest friend. Jaquobie's messengers were misinformed that the other duchies were sending emissaries." She shook her head slowly. "I really can't fathom what Duke DeLacqua is hoping to gain by inviting these people to his home. I understand that Sir Charles is here for his residency, and Lady Giovanna's performance talents will certainly be of merit, but everyone else? The Haulsingers hardly seem able to influence Duke Savant to lower the cloth tax. For all their important airs, they were actually dressed very drably."

Perry frowned at her. "Virtue's sake, what are you going on about, Jax?"

"Their clothing. I understand Lady Florence was a renowned tailor in her prime, and the clothes she and her husband wore last night spoke of elegance, but I saw fraying seams and hastily sewn patches all over their attire. Rather an odd choice for an event as sophisticated as an inaugural dinner."

"But did you see the brooch Lady Florence was wearing?"

Jax responded with a blank stare.

"I'm surprised it escaped your watchful and might I add, critical, eye," Perry said. "Although, I only noticed it myself on our way out when the lady adjusted her shawl. I'd never call myself an expert in diamonds and such, but it was massive. Diamonds, rubies, emeralds, you name it. Must have been the size of those chocolate bonbons you love to eat." Winking, Perry took her hand and led her down to the main deck. "I know our companions seem like a group of misfits, but let's give them the benefit of the doubt, Jax. Everyone was perfectly friendly last night at dinner. Well, except Sir Ernest."

Perry shuddered, and Jax, too, recalled the old man spewing bits of his meal across the table.

"You're right." She smiled. "I'm just looking for trouble, I guess. Let's find Uma and the others and head to breakfast. I'm starving."

Nodding good morning to the two guards stationed at the entrance of the passageway that led to their suites, Jax noticed Jogan briskly walking to his father's cabin up ahead, armed with a pitcher of water and a small pouch. "Good morning, Jogan!" she called. "Will the Captain be joining us for breakfast this morning?"

Jax was startled by the worried expression on the first mate's face as he turned to greet them. "Good morning, Your Grace. I hope you all slept well. Unfortunately, my father and I will be dining in his cabin today."

The Duchess frowned, curious as to why the Captain had not joined the group in last night's festivities, either. "Is everything all right, Jogan?" She hoped to get more information than the young man was letting on.

He shifted awkwardly on his feet, looking unsure of how to reply. "Well, Your Grace, I am a bit worried. Father took ill last night after he briefly attended the cocktail hour Lady Carriena hosted. At first, I thought maybe he wasn't used to sailing on this large of a ship and was having a hard time adjusting to the different movement. But then it continued on through the night, and he seems to be doing worse this morning," Jogan reported, his voice cracking near the end.

Jax and Perry exchanged worried looks. She found it hard to believe that a seaman as experienced as Captain Valhalen was suffering from seasickness. "Has the ship's doctor attended to him?" she asked.

A helpless look on his face, Jogan replied. "*Rose of the Sea* has no appointed physician at the moment. Duke DeLacqua thought that there would be no need, with both a High Priestess and an Academy resident traveling on board for its first voyage. I'm just coming back from speaking with Miss Hazel. She gave me some herbs to try." He motioned to the small leather pouch tucked under his arm.

"Goodness, then please don't let us deter you any longer," Jax said, her waving hand urging Jogan to complete his task. The young man bowed low before disappearing into his father's chambers, the door closing with a snap.

"I don't like that look on your face, Jax," Perry groaned, seeming to know what the Duchess was thinking.

But instead of replying, Jax grabbed her skirts and ran over to the outside of the Captain's door. Jogan must have placed an empty water pitcher and platter of half-eaten food out to be collected by the guards. She surveyed the remnants of the meal, her face scrunched in concentration. "We're kidding ourselves if we're going to accept this as seasickness, Perry. Hazel would have given the captain gingerroot if that was the case, not a whole bag of herbs."

Perry knelt beside her and picked up the nearly empty water jug. He brought it to his nose and sniffed, immediately cringing at whatever assaulted his senses. "What does this smell like to you?"

Jax leaned in and inhaled, a sweetly bitter aroma flourishing in her nose. Stuttering through a cough, she said through teary eyes, "Why, is almost smells like smoked nutmeg."

Perry nodded in agreement. "Very close. It's actually a plant called cloveroot. I've used it before when mixing paint. It creates a stunning midnight blue, but if ingested, it can make a person extremely ill."

Jax's eyes widened at Perry's revelation. "You mean someone used cloveroot to intentionally poison the Captain?"

Perry put down the pitcher, his face grim. "Cloveroot in small doses won't kill anyone, but as I said, they'll be in a sickbed for a few days, at least."

"You'd think he would have realized it was laced." Jax sniffed the pitcher once more, flinching.

"Cloveroot reacts with its solute over time. It would have taken hours for it to reach this intensity," Perry informed her, speaking casually, as if this was common knowledge.

"Why would anyone want to put the Captain out of commission while we're at sea? He's supposed to be navigating this blasted thing!" Jax knew Perry didn't have an answer for her, but her frustration clouded her judgment. "We must ask Jogan where this water came from. I highly doubt he's our culprit, but I'd prefer it if we were careful with our words." Not bothering to wait for Perry's consent, Jax rapped briskly on the cabin door.

A few moments later, a sliver of Jogan's face appeared; the young man was obviously hesitant to open the entry the rest of the way. "Your Grace? Did you need something else?"

Jax clasped her hands before her, watching the first mate carefully. "This might sound a bit odd, Jogan, but can you tell me where the pitcher of water outside your father's door came from? I only ask because I had hoped for some refreshments in my room and was disappointed to find none."

Jogan's cheeks erupted with panic as he flung open the door in a sweeping bow. "My sincerest apologies, Your Grace. I'll speak to the galley staff about this oversight. At the moment, I'm not really sure who would be in charge of stocking the rooms. This pitcher was here last night before my father and I headed out on deck for the cocktail hour."

"Did you drink any of the water yourself, Jogan?" Perry asked, stepping out from Jax's regal shadow.

The young man gave Perry a wary glance, obviously unsure what his question had to do with the Duchess's inquiry. "Well, no, actually. I figured I would wait to drink until the cocktail hour kicked off. Wish I had, though. Father only let us stay a few minutes before we retreated to the helm to scour star charts." Jogan looked to Jax for confirmation, and she nodded, remembering her encounter with the struggling first mate.

Suddenly, Perry reached out and took Jogan by the arm. "That reminds me, sir, there's something in my cabin I require you to examine. When I woke this morning, I could have sworn there was a sea snake in my bathtub. Hendrie and I are both quite terrified of snakes, so if you could just come see to it quickly." As he pulled the bewildered first mate down the hallway, Perry threw an urgent look Jax's way. Realizing that she was standing outside the open door of the Captain's chambers, she immediately understood that Perry had deliberately created a distraction to allow her to sneak inside and see if the water pitcher Jogan had been carrying moments ago was also laced with cloveroot.

Ducking inside the room, Jax was astonished once more by the sheer size of the cabin, which appeared to be at least three full rooms. The entryway she stood in now was cluttered with scrolls and books, a big brass telescope pointing out the western window. Perched on the edge of a worn, yet grand desk, sat the water jug and packet of herbs. Racing over, Jax took in a deep breath, exhaling relief. The bittersweet scent of cloveroot was nowhere to be found in the jug or in the jumbled packet of dried plants. Whoever had laced the Captain's water pitcher last night had not done so this morning.

Knowing there was no time to waste, Jax exited the room, although not before hearing Captain Valhalen's moans of discomfort coming from behind one of the closed doors. Even though the man had not been poisoned this morning, from what Perry had told her, Valhalen was still in for a world of hurt and would spend the next few days recovering.

Stopping herself from shutting the door, as Jogan had left it ajar, Jax tried to look casual as she stood in the hallway when Perry and the first mate emerged from the Emerald Suite. "I'm sorry, ol' chap," Perry said to Jogan as the pair strode back to the Captain's Cabin. "I could have sworn there was something there this morning. I hope this doesn't mean there's a sea snake loose on the boat." He chuckled, then turned to Jax. "Well, Duchess, I think we have bothered Master Jogan here long enough. Shall we head to breakfast?"

Bidding the slightly flustered first mate a demure goodbye, Jax reached for Perry's arm and they retraced their steps to the dining hall. "The water Jogan brought this morning was not tampered with," Jax whispered as they walked across the main deck. "Do you think this all could have been an accident?"

Perry frowned. "No cook worth his salt would keep cloveroot lying around. The risks are far too great."

"Then we must be mindful of our traveling companions, Perry. Any one of them could have orchestrated this," Jax murmured as they entered the rowdy room, already full of morning chatter. "I know the guards are not supposed to let anyone but our delegation, Carriena, Jogan, and Valhalen through the suite entrance, but with all the commotion of yesterday's departure, I wouldn't be surprised if someone was able to sneak in without being seen and lace the water pitcher."

"Well, I'll see if I can dig anything up," Perry said as he gave her a quick peck on the cheek. As charming as he was, Jax blushed at the breach in protocol, especially in front of a room of relative strangers. He recognized his mistake right away and sheepishly pointed to the table. "I think I see a cherry tart with your name on it." With that, he strolled over with renewed confidence to Hazel and Vincent Quorimander, engaging them in conversation.

Jax took in the crowd and spotted Carriena speaking to Lady Giovanna. Her friend's earnest expression and demure stance, hands clasped in front of her, suggested Carriena was offering an apology. Approaching the two women, Jax smiled in greeting.

"Oh, Duchess, there you are," Carriena said as she noticed Jax. "I was just about ready to send Uma after you. She was an absolute treasure, helping me out last night. Goodness, I was in a bit of a state. Thank you for having her stay with me. I was telling Lady Giovanna how sorry I am to have put her on the spot in front of everyone." Her words rushed out in a breathless fashion, her eyes bright and alert, the remnants of last night's honeyed mead long gone.

"And I was telling our hostess that I would be honored to perform this evening, if that suits Her Highness." Lady Giovanna bowed her head to Carriena, clearly intimidated by the woman's commanding presence.

"I would be delighted, and I'm sure everyone on board will be thrilled." Carriena paused, looking around. "Is your brother joining us for breakfast?"

Lady Giovanna glanced over her shoulder in the direction of the entryway. "He was right behind me a moment ago. He must have forgotten something and gone back to his cabin."

Jax followed the young woman's gaze, noticing that Charles was not the only guest not yet in the dining room. Lady Florence and Master Archer were also not among them at the moment.

"Well, I invite you to tuck in. The candied toast is particularly good." Carriena motioned for Jax and Giovanna to take their seats at the table, and Jax's eyes were immediately drawn to the sugar-and-pecan crusted, syrup laden bread.

Chuckling, Jax said, "Goodness, who would have thought we'd eat so well this far out at sea. I feared that I'd be stuck eating smoked cod this entire voyage." She hoped to engage the quiet Lady Giovanna in conversation. She had not spoken to the young woman as much as she would have liked to last night, considering her realm-renowned talents.

"I'll have to pace myself or I won't be able to fit into any of my costumes back home." The actress smiled conspiratorially at Jax.

"How long do you plan to stay on Isla DeLacqua once we make port?" Jax asked, hastily swallowing a mouthful of cherry tart.

"Not very long. I'll help my brother get settled, and I have a few performances for the royal court scheduled in honor of Lady Carriena's birthday, but I hope to travel back to Hestes within a fortnight or so," Giovanna responded modestly.

"I do hope you'll consider bringing your talents to Saphire in the near future. Many of our noble houses would be astounded by your voice. It brought me to tears when I last heard it," Jax said.

Giovanna's cheeks blossomed into pink petals. "You're too kind, Your Grace. It would be an honor for me, and my father as well, to perform his work for your duchy."

Pleased with the woman's acceptance of her offer, Jax's attention was momentarily diverted as Charles and Master Archer entered the room, both appearing out of sorts. Charles's face was flush, just like his sister's, and Archer's brow was drawn tight. Neither man spoke to one another as they briskly marched into the room, Archer taking a seat at the far end of the table near Uma and Hendrie, Charles sitting directly across from his sister.

Jax was about to make a comment when Perry's hand landed on her shoulder, his mouth whispering in her ear. "Our friends from Zaltor are either very skilled in deception or they are innocent. I asked Hazel if she carried cloveroot with her, as I needed some to mix up some paints. Not only did she not have any, but she told me how dangerous it is to carry cloveroot around. She knows its poisonous properties, indeed, but her reprimand was far too real, in my opinion, for her to be the culprit."

With the slightest tilt of her head, Jax surveyed the two Zaltorians. "What about Vincent?"

"He didn't say much, but his expression makes me believe in his innocence as well," Perry shared with conviction.

As much as she wanted to agree with Perry, the stoic nature of the two Ancient Faith practitioners made Jax uneasy. She'd encountered enough people in the past who'd been skillful liars to be hesitant to discount them entirely, especially since Hazel knew of the poisonous side effects of the root. She was about to say as much to Perry, when a loud wail from the door took the whole room off guard.

"My brooch! My brooch is gone!" Lady Florence burst into the dining hall, all grace and decorum thrown aside as she cried in despair. Her gray hair looked as though she had torn it out in panic, her face streaked with tears.

Carriena was by the woman's side first, taking a trembling hand in her own. "Lady Florence, please calm down or you will faint. What's this about your brooch?"

"My jeweled clip," the old woman gasped, clutching her chest. "I wore it to dinner last night and put it in my jewelry box before I went to bed. As I was leaving my chambers for breakfast, I went to put it on and it was gone! It has been stolen!"

Jax pushed her chair back from the table, abandoning her untouched candied toast. "Lady Florence, perhaps you misplaced the brooch. Have you searched your room thoroughly for the piece?"

Florence turned a hostile glare on Jax. "Oh, you think that because I'm almost three times your age that I forgot where I put my family's most treasured heirloom?" she snapped, her cloudy eyes wild with panic.

Jax was momentarily affronted at being addressed in such a chilling manner, but quickly recovered. "I didn't mean to imply anything regarding your age, Lady Florence. We all drank a bit too much mead last night, and I was simply asking whether or not your entire cabin had been thoroughly searched."

"I know that I placed the brooch in my jewelry box last night. Unlike some people here, I can hold my liquor, thank you very much," Lady Florence barked back, judgment lacing her words.

"Was anything else stolen from your jewelry box?" Perry asked, calmly directing the line of questioning back on track from his position behind Jax's abandoned chair.

The old woman looked at him for a moment. "No, it hardly looks like the box was disturbed at all, except for the gaping spot where my beloved brooch used to be." She turned around to face Carriena. "I demand all the ships' servants be searched at once. One of those grubby hands likely nicked it." Her eyes searched the room, maliciously landing on Uma and Hendrie. "And those two, as well. The Saphire servants."

Jax's temper flared, and her amethyst eyes darkened with anger. "No one from the Saphire delegation would take your heirloom, ma'am. As Duchess, Uma and Hendrie are under my protection and will not be subjected to your hysterical whims." Her voice simmered with cold fury.

Carriena shot a pleading look at Jax, begging her not to send the woman over the precarious edge she was balancing on. "I will see to it personally that the servants who had access to your chambers are interviewed, Lady Florence. Please, sit down and have some tea while I go speak with the Captain."

Carriena handed Florence off to the awaiting arm of Master Archer, who escorted the lady to an empty seat by her husband, who, to Jax's surprise and bewilderment, was fast asleep, butter dribbling down his chin.

Sharing a look amongst themselves, Carriena, Jax, and Perry retreated into the hallway, quickly joined by Uma, Hendrie, and George.

"This is a nightmare!" Carriena wrung her hands. "What are we going to do? That old bat will make the rest of this trip miserable if we don't find her clip. I must go speak with Captain Valhalen immediately."

"That might be a bit tricky, my dear." Jax bit her lip as Carriena turned to her with confused eyes. She and Perry quickly explained to the small group about the Captain's illness, which was a result of cloveroot-laced water.

"Are you both in agreement that these two incidences are related?" George asked, looking at both Jax and Perry for guidance.

"It seems a bit too much of a coincidence that our captain is poisoned, then a valuable piece of jewelry goes missing within the span of twelve hours," Jax surmised, seeing Perry nod his head from the corner of her eye. "Although, I'm still not convinced the brooch is actually missing. I'd like to poke around her room and see for myself, if possible." She looked at her hostess, who nodded swiftly.

"Lady Carriena, I will go with you to speak with Jogan about this incident," George stated, offering his arm to escort the young woman to the upper deck cabins.

"I'll head back into the dining room and keep an eye on things," Perry said. "I'm curious as to how the guests are reacting to this strange new development."

"Perfect. Uma, Hendrie, and I will go to Lady Florence's cabin, then," Jax said, looking to the valet and lady's maid.

"There are two sentries keeping watch over the door leading to the lower cabins. They'll be able to show you which room is hers," Carriena explained before taking off with George.

"Good luck." Perry winked as he ducked back into the dining hall, a momentary surge of commotion sliding through the crack of the opened door.

Jax turned to Hendrie and Uma, noticing their faces had become extremely pale. "I want you two to pay absolutely no mind to that horrible woman's accusations. You are not merely Saphire servants, you know that, right? You are trusted companions of the Duchess and her household. If it was up to me, I'd have that woman locked up. It's a direct order from your sovereign that you forget what she said." Clasping their hands to express her conviction, she waited until they nodded acceptance. "Now, let's see what trouble we've come up against this time."

Chapter Four

"Her room is second to last on the portside," the smaller of the guards said as he escorted the inquisitive group down the long corridor of the lower deck. In his hands, he held a piece of parchment, which Jax spied to be a manifest, mapping out which guest occupied each of the ten rooms. The first two to the right and left of the entryway were empty, according to the list. "Her husband's room is two down from hers." The young man pointed to the brass plate that bore the number seven. "I swear on my own life that no one entered her room while Ferdinand and I were on duty, Your Grace. We've been here since around three this morning." The man's muddy brown eyes shone with sincerity.

"Thank you, Diego," Jax said with a graceful smile. "And there is no other way for someone to access her room?"

"Her room? No, Your Grace. Lady Florence was not given a cabin with a balcony. I suppose if someone *really* wanted to, they could get into one of the cabins with an attached balcony by entering from the outer door. But, as I said, her room does not have one." Diego was trembling, obviously nervous under the circumstances; a sea-bound guardsman was not normally interrogated by a foreign Duchess.

Intrigued by what she had heard so far, Jax motioned for Diego to unlock the cabin door. "Are there many master keys aboard the ship?" she asked quietly.

Diego shook his head. "We have one master key that is handed off to the next guards on shift. The Captain also has one. But other than the passenger's own key, that's it."

Jax made a note to confirm that Captain Valhalen or Jogan were still in possession of a master key. "Did anyone need assistance getting into their rooms last night?"

"I'm sorry, Your Grace, but everyone had already retired to their cabins by the time Ferdinand and I arrived on shift. You might ask Sebastián and Eduardo when they wake up. They would have been on watch at that point," Diego explained.

"Are there any others we could speak with?" Hendrie asked.

"Ferdinand and I monitor the lower cabins until three in the afternoon, which is when Sebastián and Eduardo come back. The only others are the boys watching your suites on the upper deck. Ian and Isaac in daytime, and Alonso and Felipe at night." Diego mapped out the guards' scheduled rotation.

"You've been so helpful, Diego. We'll take it from here." Jax smiled sweetly to the young man once more before pushing open the door to Lady Florence's chambers. At once, Jax was put off by the small size of the compartment. Spoiled by the regality of her own suite, she was surprised that this appeared to be a rather common-looking cabin, despite being on the realm's most luxurious vessel. With only space for a bed, a small loveseat, a desk, and tea table, the room was nevertheless decorated tastefully. A small door on the left wall opened into a pristinely white bathroom, with only a few bottles cluttering the hand washing basin.

Lady Florence's panic over the missing heirloom was evident in the chaotic state of the cabin. The bedsheets had been ransacked and clothes had been tossed carelessly onto the floor. "It doesn't appear that the maid service has come by her room yet," Jax noted.

"Both guards said no one had been in the corridor this morning other than the guests themselves." Hendrie reminded her.

"Here's the jewelry box," Jax said, her eyes narrowing in on a small vanity in the corner. The large wooden box was expertly polished; her reflection gleamed back at her as she approached. Lifting off the gold-rimmed top, she peered curiously at the contents.

To anyone other than a Duchess, the fine jewels may have left them in awe, but Jax was hardly impressed by the old woman's collection. Drop pearl earrings and silver necklaces snaked along the sides of the box, a ruby locket on a gold chain coiled along the center. The glaring absence of a signature piece was evident, a large hole announcing where the clip had once rested. "Well, the brooch is definitely not in this box," Jax confirmed, shutting the lid with a snap. "Any sign of it elsewhere?"

Hendrie was on his knees, looking under the loveseat and bed, while Uma raked her delicate hands under the bedsheets, looking to see if the piece was tucked away in the mattress. "As rude as she was, she unfortunately was right about one thing. Her brooch isn't here, Your Grace," Uma said with a sigh, placing her hands on her hips, surveying the last inches of the room.

Jax's brow wrinkled as she scowled in concentration. "If someone was going to steal something, why not try for one of *my* crowns or jewels?"

Hendrie stood up from the floor, rubbing non-existent dirt from his pants. "Perhaps the risk was too great?"

"Why? Both the upper deck and lower deck rooms were guarded, and we already know that someone was able to get cloveroot into Captain Valhalen's cabin," Jax pointed out.

"Do you know for certain that someone snuck into the Captain's quarters and laced his water? Or is it possible that they added the cloveroot in the ship's galley?" Uma asked, twisting her lower lip as she timidly pushed back on her sovereign's theory.

The Duchess paused as she considered Uma's words. "I suppose you could be right. We really don't know how or even when the Captain was poisoned. Yet, somehow cloveroot ended up in a pitcher in the man's room." She looked at her two companions, their faces a mask of unease. "We will need to be extremely careful going forward. Uma, I hate to ask more of you, but for now, until this nastiness is resolved, I'd like you to personally bring my water to me. You are not to accept water from anyone other than the barrels they come from. Hendrie, I'd like you to do the same for Lord Pettraud. At meals, we will only begin eating after the other guests have started, ensuring that no one in the Saphire party ingests something that no one else hasn't already tried."

If either felt put off by their Duchess's commands, they did not display it. Uma and Hendrie bowed low to Jax before retreating from the room. Hendrie turned to say, "We'll go to the kitchens right away, Duchess, and secure some water for this afternoon."

"Wonderful. Be careful, you two." Jax gave them a matronly nod before setting course to return to the main deck. No doubt breakfast had, by now, concluded and the guests were beginning to settle into late-morning activities. She bid Ferdinand and Diego goodbye, encouraging them to come speak to her or Captain Solomon directly if they saw anything of note. She would seek out Sebastián and Eduardo when they returned to their posts.

The brilliant morning sun caressed her face as she stepped onto the main deck, surveying the scene. Carriena and George were not among the passengers, probably still speaking with Jogan. Perry, too, was nowhere to be seen. The Montivarius siblings were playing a card game with Monsieur Grandeair, while Hazel and Archer lounged near the portside railing, reading. Vincent simply paced around the deck, trying to avoid the deadly looks Lady Florence was shooting him and the other guests. She and her husband sat in the shade near the dining hall's entrance, glowering at the world, likely watching the upper deck doorway for Lady Carriena's return.

Jax floated gracefully over to the High Priestess and Master Builder, the shuffle of her skirts pulling their attention away from their books. "Don't tell me this ship has a library, as well?" she asked with mock surprise.

Hazel merely smiled at the joke, but Archer burst into raucous laughter. Jax smirked inwardly. She hadn't been *that* funny.

"I believe I forgot to add a library when I was drawing up the plans for the *Rose*, Duquessa." Archer stood up from the quilted lounge chair, offering Jax his spot.

She shook her head, a feigned flirtatious smile struggling on her lips. "I'm afraid I've spent too much of my time reading boring political documents and scrolls to want to read for pleasure on this glorious day. I just wanted to check in to make sure everyone had calmed down after this morning's outburst." Jax tilted her head toward Lady Florence's foreboding figure.

Hazel straightened in her chair. "I gave her some herbal tea to help placate her nerves. She was in quite a state, indeed."

"You'd think a little brooch would hardly be a drop in the bucket for a noble house such as the Haulsingers," Archer commented, giving Jax a charming, yet snide, look.

Jax bit her tongue, remembering the lackluster assortment of jewelry the old woman kept hidden away. Normally, Jax would have agreed with Master Archer's assessment about the noble class, but Lady Florence's hysterics told Jax this piece was more valuable than anything else in the old woman's possession. How she wished she had spotted it last night at dinner. "Lady Hazel, are you concerned that this may affect her health further?"

The High Priestess's fire-yellow eyes appraised Jax momentarily before she responded with finesse, "I believe the shock of the incident has run its course. She's in relatively good health for her age, so I do not think she's in any danger."

"That's good to hear," Jax said. "Her room has been thoroughly searched and the brooch is indeed gone. However, there was nothing to suggest an intruder in the cabin, so we have very little to go on."

"So it is true, what they say," Hazel said, her smooth voice followed by a tight smile, "the Duchess of Saphire does like to dabble in detecting the truth." Her stoic expression revealed little else about her statement.

Jax's cheeks reddened, not realizing word of her past adventures had reached the deserts of the realm. "I am a proponent of justice, that's all, High Priestess."

From the look on his face, Master Archer appeared to not follow the line of conversation. "So, I take it the jewel is lost?"

Jax directed her gaze to the ship's builder. "For now, yes. Master Archer, would there be any way for someone to enter the cabins other than through a door?"

Her question clearly puzzled him. "Are you asking if I built any secret passages in the *Rose?*"

Jax continued to stare at him, waiting for him to work it out himself.

Closing his book with a snap, he paced around the chairs. "Nothing was built into the lower cabins that would constitute a passage. On the upper deck, the suites are connected by a series of hidden hallways, designed to allow servants to travel between the rooms without crowding the corridor. They're not in use yet, as this ship currently is not at full staff." He stopped roaming around and turned to Jax. "No, I can think of no other way for a person to enter the lower deck rooms."

Inwardly, Jax cursed. How in the name of the Virtues did someone get into Lady Florence's room without the guards seeing anything? She needed to speak with Sebastián and Eduardo immediately. "Well, thank you for the stimulating conversation. I'll leave you both to your reading." Jax didn't wait for a reply as she turned on her heel, her eyes narrowing in on the two guards surveying the upper deck entrance. If she remembered Diego correctly, the two daytime guards were Ian and Isaac. "Excuse me, gentlemen," she said as she approached the alert guardsmen, "would you mind pointing me in the direction of where I can find the off-duty sentries? I'd like to speak to them about my continued safety, considering last night's events." While Jax was not immediately concerned for herself, she figured it was a more plausible reason to speak with the guardsmen. Hazel had already surmised she was investigating the incident, but Jax preferred her own inquiry be kept secret as much as possible. She didn't need a larger target on her back.

"Your Grace, surely we can summon them for you," the rounder of the guards replied, not disguising his incredulity.

Jax shook her head daintily. "No, that's quite all right. I haven't had much time to explore the ship, so I'd like to take a look around."

Exchanging uncomfortable looks, the other guard directed her. "There's a small entryway tucked under the stairs to the bow, just before the entrance to the dining area. Follow them down a hallway and our quarters will be to starboard."

Thanking the two men, Jax proceeded to follow their instructions and found herself descending a dark, tight set of stairs taking her deep into the belly of the ship. A long corridor stretched before her as she reached the bottom, sounds and smells of the galley coming from the first archway on the right. Peering inside to catch a glimpse of the kitchen, Jax was mesmerized by the long, slim window, revealing a peek at the whitecaps of the sea. Designed to keep the galley cool and smoke-free, Jax noticed a lengthy wooden panel hovering above the lip of the window, which she guessed was used as cover if the level of the water swelled past the bottom of the window. That was how Master Archer was able to design a cool and comfortable galley below deck. Though smaller than her kitchens back home, *Rose of the Sea* certainly had adequate quarters for cooking. An unattended pot bubbled over the hearth, the smells of lunch floating through her nostrils.

Pulling herself away from the distracting sight, Jax meandered down the rest of the hallway, passing closed door after door. Finally, she arrived at the last door on the right and knocked. The young men who were on watch last night were likely still sleeping, but she needed her questions answered.

After a few more incessant knocks, the door whipped open, a sleepy-eyed, brown-haired man yawning in her face. "I'm looking for Sebastián and Eduardo, please," she stated, waiting for the young guard to focus in on her.

"I'm Eduardo, what do you want?" he retorted, his eyes still glassy. She stood silently for a moment, watching recognition dawn across his face. "Duchess! Virtues' sake, please forgive me! What are you doing down here?" His mortification at his behavior was at war with his curiosity as to her presence.

Jax calmly reassured him. "Eduardo, please, nothing to forgive. I'm sorry to disturb you, but I have a few important questions I must ask. Have you heard about what happened last night?"

"What's happened?" Immediate panic settled in the man's brown eyes.

"Nothing terrible. It's just that a precious heirloom was stolen from one of the guests," Jax explained, mindfully monitoring his reaction.

Quick relief flooded his face before a furrowed brow appeared. "Which guest? Do you know what was stolen?"

"Well, it appears that Lady Florence Haulsinger was in possession of a jeweled brooch that is worth quite a sum in gold and emotional value. There are witnesses confirming that she was wearing it at dinner last night, and this morning when she woke, it was gone from her chambers."

Eduardo took in Jax's description and pondered it silently for a few minutes. "Well, I remember when everyone came back from dinner. It was just past midnight by the time the last guest entered their cabin. I'll wake Sebastián to confirm, but no one came out of their rooms once they went in. At least, not during our shift."

Jax stepped forward, urgency fueling her actions. "What time did you switch shifts with Diego and Ferdinand? Could someone have entered Lady Florence's room during that point?"

Eduardo shifted uncomfortably on his feet, rubbing a hand on the back of his neck. "Well, they took over at about three in the morning. We chatted a few moments about our observations from the night, but I hardly think we were distracted enough to not notice anyone moving about the hallway."

"But it is possible someone could have slipped quickly into her room without you noticing?" Jax prodded further.

"I mean, I suppose it's not impossible, Your Grace, but they still would have had to come back out at some point. From the sounds of it, you've already spoken with Diego and Ferdinand. Did they see anyone come out of the room?" Eduardo countered.

Jax shook her head, her shoulders slumping. "No, they saw nothing either." She stared off into the darkness of the corridor's end, contemplating her next move. "If Lady Florence hadn't been so adamant that she put the brooch back in her jewelry box last night, I would be inclined to think she simply dropped it on the way back to her room. It's like a phantom whisked it away."

Eduardo bit his lip before backing away from the door. "Let me get Sebastián up. Perhaps he has something else that may help."

But Sebastián's story mirrored Eduardo's perfectly. As Jax left the two young men to return to their slumber, she ran through the scenario over and over again. While she trusted the word of the two guards that they didn't see anything, the only possible time someone could have entered Lady Florence's room was during the shift change. Perhaps all the men were afraid to admit a misstep and had seen something, or had their attention diverted from the rooms for just long enough. But until she learned otherwise, she didn't know how to proceed.

Grimacing to herself at her dark thoughts, she stepped out into the midday sun, hidden for the moment behind some brewing clouds. Gazing at the foreboding sky, she murmured, "Maybe it was a phantom, after all."

Chapter Five

A subdued mood hung over the room like a cobweb, everyone settling down into dinner after a seemingly endless day. Jax couldn't remember the last time she had this much free time on her hands, and she was already getting antsy, anxious to be back on land. She'd spoken with Jogan just before dinner, and the young man confirmed that the second copy of the ship's master key was in his possession. While she was relieved the key had not been stolen, it complicated the puzzle of the brooch's theft even more.

The sun's rays had beaten off the threatening clouds, its victory evident in the glowing red of Charles and Giovanna's pale skin. Uma and Hendrie, too, had a pink hue about them, leaving Jax relieved she had sought shelter in the shade.

Lady Carriena did not bother with a toast this evening, signaling her guests to start their meal. Jax could tell her friend was particularly unsettled by the news of the Captain's illness, as it seemed to shroud a sinister veil over the voyage. George had spent much of the day questioning the ship's crew and staff, failing to find out any additional information regarding the stolen brooch. "There's a skilled liar among us," he had seethed earlier in the afternoon when recounting his conversations to Jax and Perry.

Watching the group dig into their steaming meals of asparagus and roast beef, Jax slid a knowing look down the table to where

George, Uma, and Hendrie sat, waiting for her signal. Ernest Haulsinger gobbled down nearly half his plate before she secretly nodded that it was safe for the Saphire group to begin their meal. Across from her, Perry picked up his fork and pierced the juicy red meat with enthusiasm.

"Lady Carriena, if it would please you and the rest of the table, I would love to sing a new song from my father's latest production," Giovanna said meekly, breaking the strained silence.

Carriena smiled, relief flooding her face. "That would be an absolute delight, my dear. Yes, I think some music would do us all a bit of good. Lift the spirits, and such." Glancing around, she was met with fervent nods of agreement.

"So, we're just going to be mindlessly entertained while my brooch remains lost?" Lady Florence's sharp voice cut through the brightening mood. Her cheeks were as red as her dark evening gown, a piece that was well-put together, more so than her previous night's ensemble.

A muscle in Carriena's jaw tightened in obvious annoyance. "Lady Florence, please rest assured that we are actively looking into the disappearance of your clip, but please have some compassion for your fellow travelers and let them enjoy themselves a bit."

"Oh, excuse me for my misfortune ruining this cruise for the rest of you." The old woman burst to her feet, throwing her napkin down. "This voyage is cursed, if you ask me."

Watching Florence hobble out of the room in a rage, Jax contemplated the woman's exclamation. A lost brooch was hardly reason to call a voyage cursed, but the poisoning of the Captain did worry the Duchess that *Rose of the Sea* was not poised for smooth sailing.

"Pay no attention to the woman; she's hysterical. The brooch was ugly, anyway," Ernest grumbled, drowning his second helping of beef in a thick, murky gravy.

Jax forced herself to restrain an eye roll. Regardless of his wife's outburst, she found Ernest's display just as distasteful. "I, for one, am looking forward to hearing you perform, Lady Giovanna," she commented, drawing the room's attention back to the table.

Jax was startled when, about to enter the ballroom to listen to the musical performance, Carriena's hand gripped tightly around her wrist. "Jax, may I have a word?"

"Of course, what is it?" Jax's heart grew heavy with worry, sensing all was not well with her friend.

"I could overlook Lady Florence's missing brooch as bad luck, but after learning Captain Valhalen has been poisoned, I'm beginning to think someone is trying to sabotage my success as hostess." Carriena wrung her hands, the jewels on her fingers sparkling with menace in the low candlelight. "If the other guests feel they are not safe enough aboard this ship, how will I ever convince them to partner with Isla DeLacqua?"

Jax, not having have an immediate answer, bit her lip in silence.

"I need your help to figure out whatever is going on here," Carriena pleaded. "I know the guardsmen on board should be looking into it, but they don't have your experience with this type of thing."

Jax blushed. "My experience? It's mostly been just luck."

Carriena shook her head, her eyes brimming with fierce loyalty. "No, I know you better than anyone in your present company. You are smart and you are clever. You can get to the bottom of this, I just know it."

"Of course I'll help, Carriena. But I'm afraid that the little digging I've already done has not turned up much," Jax admitted.

Carriena cringed. "Well, I pray the Virtues watch over the remaining voyage. Jogan said we should make port within three more days if the winds hold strong."

"That's wonderful to hear," Jax said. "Why don't you retire early this evening, my dear? You look a bit worn out from everything."

Looking down the hall into the grand ballroom, the young woman nodded, a wall of sadness behind her royal eyes. "I think you're right. I'll see you in the morning, Jax."

Giving Carriena a quick hug goodnight, Jax grabbed her skirts and rushed down to the entrance of the ballroom, eager to listen to Lady Giovanna's performance. Barely taking in the immaculately polished wooden floors and breathtaking chandelier that hung from the center of the room, Jax spotted an empty seat next to Perry.

"What was that about?" he murmured, leaning in closely so they were not overheard.

"Carriena wants me to figure out if there's some sort of plot to sabotage this journey," Jax whispered, cautious of the other ears around them.

"Well, knowing you, you've already said yes, but Jax, darling, you need to be careful. Stealing a brooch is one thing, but the state our captain is in is most troubling. I don't want anything happening to you." He placed a warm hand over hers, lifting it to his lips with tenderness.

"I promise." She smiled, and her cheeks deepened in color as a tingle ran through her.

Their attention was drawn away by Giovanna's innocent, melodic voice, light as a bird but with the power of a gale. Jax sat mesmerized, stunned that such a small figure could house such a strong voice. The assembled crowd responded so passionately at the song's end that Giovanna launched into another melody, this one a haunting tune.

Pulling her gaze away from the striking performance, Jax surveyed the rest of the guests. Hazel and Vincent held hands, absentmindedly stroking their fingers with love. Ernest, surprisingly, was watching Giovanna with rapt attention, although Jax shivered at the way the old man's eyes lingered on the girl's trim waist. Archer and Charles sat beside one another, Archer clearly smitten with Charles's sister. The scowl on the young physician's face told Jax that he, too, was aware of the builder's affection and not pleased by it.

George Solomon stood in the back of the room by the doorway, keeping watch over the scene. Uma and Hendrie appeared to be enjoying the music, as well as each other's company, something that immensely pleased Jax as she witnessed it. Only Monsieur Grandeair appeared to be mildly uncomfortable, his seasickness no doubt returning here in the windowless belly of the ship. He wiped his glistening forehead once more with the embroidered Cetachi handkerchief. Pitying the poor man, Jax turned her attention back to Giovanna, who finished the ballad on a beautiful, long note. Through the enthusiastic applause, Jax heard the ballroom door snap shut. A quick glance told her Monsieur Grandeair had left, George giving her an affirmative nod as she looked to him for confirmation. The sea had bested the banker for the evening, it seemed.

Giovanna performed a few more songs before announcing that she was going to return to her bedchambers. Thanking everyone for their kind words, she was escorted out by her brother. The ballroom emptied in their wake. Jax and her party bid goodnight to the others as they took the staircase leading to the upper deck suites.

As much as she enjoyed the evening's entertainment, Jax was glad to have the day behind her. Running through the events since their departure from Tandora's harbor, she fell into an uneven sleep, dreaming about the dark sea thrashing below.

Chapter Six

Jax and Uma were the first to arrive in the dining hall the following morning, as the Duchess was eager to observe her fellow passengers as they entered. With Uma watching from her seat further down the table, Jax kept a close eye on the door. She was surprised to see Lady Florence and Master Archer enter together, laughing. The old woman spotted Jax and Uma and immediately turned her attention to them. "I owe you both a sincere apology for my behavior thus far. Uma, dear, I was wrong to suggest you might be involved with the disappearance of my brooch, and I very much regret my outburst last night. By the time I arrived at my room and sat down for a bit, I realized how childish I was being. A brooch, even a dear heirloom, is simply a brooch."

Master Archer patted her hand with assurance. "She even came out as we all returned from Lady Giovanna's performance to apologize last night."

Jax smiled tightly at the woman, accepting her words with grace, although not entirely putting to bed her feelings of displeasure. Uma, however, appeared to have forgiven Lady Florence for her previous slight, and offered the seat next to her as a peace offering. Jax smirked. Uma was much kinder than she'd ever be.

Hazel and Vincent entered next, bidding everyone a warm good morning, followed by Charles and Giovanna. Carriena glided into the room on the arm of Captain Solomon, Perry and Hendrie right behind them. The group settled into their seats, conversation already much livelier than it had been the previous day. Only Jax seemed to notice that Monsieur Grandeair was absent from the table. Frowning, she hoped the man's seasickness had not gotten the better of him already.

Carriena leaned over, whispering in her ear. "I ran into Jogan on my way down. It seems the Captain is making a fast recovery. He should be back on his feet by tomorrow."

"What a relief," Jax breathed, although a darkness in Carriena's eyes stopped her. "Is something else the matter?"

Carriena surveyed the table quickly before turning back to her friend. "It's just that Jogan said the wind has died down significantly. No one else has seemed to catch on yet, but we are not really moving, just rocking in the sea."

Processing Carriena's words, Jax took a moment to focus on the ship's jerky rhythm, cursing her obliviousness. The steady sailing of the vessel was gone, replaced by a barely noticeable swaying. Perhaps if she was on the main or top deck, it would have been apparent, but she'd been in the dining hall for most of the hour. "What does that mean for our voyage?"

"Well," Carriena replied, pausing to bite her lower lip, "it means we are stuck here until the wind picks up."

"Does Jogan know when that will be?" A small burst of panic flooded Jax's chest. She found the thought of being stranded at sea incredibly daunting. She suddenly wanted off of this boat.

"No." Carriena shook her head. "All we can do is pray to the Virtues that the wind is restored soon."

Jax placed her napkin over her platter, no longer hungry for the custard pie that sat atop it, covered in sugary syrup. Taking a look around the table, she felt jittery with worry. Perhaps the stagnant air was the cause of Monsieur Grandeair's absence from the breakfast table. "We should probably go check on the banker, my dear. With the boat rocking back and forth like this, he might be in serious discomfort."

Carriena looked surprised at her suggestion. "Goodness, I didn't even realize he was missing. Bit of a non-event, isn't he? I'll keep everyone in good spirits here; the longer they realize we're not moving, the better. Why don't you and Perry go check on him? Maybe make a romantic stroll out of it?" Her eyebrows wiggled suggestively, causing the Duchess to roll her eyes.

"Lord Pettraud, may I borrow you for a moment?" Jax cleared her throat, pulling Perry's attention away from a Zaltorian story Vincent was telling.

Perry promptly excused himself and followed Jax out of the room. "What's this about?" His brow furrowed.

Jax explained Carriena's news that they were stranded without the wind's power, as well as her concern for Monsieur Grandeair. She was relieved when Perry, too, appeared troubled by this latest development. "The thought of being out here in the middle of the sea makes me feel like a prisoner," the young lord said with a shudder, and Jax had no doubt her future consort was remembering the time when he had briefly been imprisoned in a palace dungeon.

"It certainly will dampen the festive mood that's returned to our companions," Jax commented as she headed toward the lower deck. After bidding good morning to Diego and Ferdinand, who were once again on duty, she and Perry walked down the dimly lit hall, the sconces flickering with a strange menace. Recalling the manifest Diego had shown her yesterday, she knew Monsieur Grandeair's room was the last room on the left, just next to Lady Florence. Knocking rapidly on the door marked with a brass number nine, she waited, with no response. Perry leaned in from behind her and rapped his knuckles more harshly against the door, eliciting the same silent reply.

Jax retreated to the entrance, where Diego and Ferdinand stood at attention. "By any chance, did Monsieur Grandeair leave his cabin this morning?"

Both guards shook their heads with certainty. "No, Your Grace. His door has been shut since he went in last night."

Thanking them, Jax retraced her steps down the long passageway.

"Perhaps the old chap went back to sleep?" Perry offered, although it seemed like a halfhearted answer.

"I'm worried, Perry. He looked very sick last night; he might need a healer's attention." Jax placed her hand on the brass doorknob. "It's unlocked!" Without waiting for Perry to stop her, Jax pushed the door inward, her eyes widening.

Her hand flew up to her gaping mouth, stifling a petite shriek as she took in the sight before her. Sprawled face-down, still in his dinner jacket from last night's meal, was Monsieur Grandeair. Blood flowered from jagged holes in his shirt, pooling at the base of his back. Jax didn't need to be any closer to know the poor man had been dead for hours.

"Good grief, what in the Virtues happened here?" Perry said with a gasp as he entered the room, his pale lavender eyes round with horror.

Filled with trepidation, Jax backed away from the body, trying to come to terms with what she was seeing. It looked like the man had been stabbed multiple times, but she didn't dare get any closer to examine the wounds. The smell of death was already raging against the fresh sea air, making the small amount of custard pie in her stomach toss over repeatedly. "We must remain calm, Perry. The murderer has to still be on board."

"Are you suggesting we keep this to ourselves?" Perry's voice cracked with shock.

Jax shook her head, leaning into his tall frame. "No, but we don't want to cause an immediate panic amongst the guests and crew. This could ruin Carriena politically if word gets out that one of her guests was murdered while on board." She looked around the room for any sign as to why this happened. "Carriena can make the announcement of the man's passing, and we can hope that everyone will assume he died in his sleep."

"But the murderer will know that's not true," Perry protested. "You're putting yourself in danger by keeping this a secret. If everyone knows to be on the lookout for a killer, he or she may not retaliate for fear of being discovered," he said, his voice stern.

Jax debated choosing her own security over that of her friend's well-being. "Do you think we can trust either Charles or Hazel to examine the body for us?"

"Are you asking me if I think either of those two is capable of murder?" Perry raised an eyebrow.

Jax thought back to each guest sitting around the dining table, not quite able to believe that one of them could be a killer. "Yes, I suppose I am."

Perry stroked his cheek thoughtfully with his thumb. "If you're making me choose between the two of them, I'd say Hazel is least likely to be our culprit. As a High Priestess, she's supposed to be of impeccable moral character."

"Yet, she also knows more about herbs and natural remedies than Charles would," Jax countered.

At this, Perry looked momentarily confused. "You think whoever killed Monsieur Grandeair also poisoned Valhalen?" He folded his arms over his chest. "Quite the crime spree our killer seems to be racking up."

Jax looked down at the crumpled figure, her face registering as oddly cold. "I think this all has to do with the missing brooch. By poisoning the Captain, the thief ensured that the ship's passengers were preoccupied. And while we didn't make it public knowledge, our little group was certainly focused on the man's assailant. The thief was able to sneak into Lady Florence's room right under our noses. But I think Monsieur Grandeair saw who took the brooch and was killed to keep silent."

She could see in Perry's eyes that he did not quite share her theory. "If the guards did not see anyone enter or leave this room, how did Monsieur Grandeair become witness to the crime?"

Jax's gaze fell on the door leading out to the small terrace attached to the banker's cabin. "Maybe he was out on the balcony, hoping the fresh air would help his seasickness, and saw something. His room is right next to Lady Florence's." Without waiting for Perry to object, she flung open the outer door, a burst of sea air whipping inside the dark quarters. Stepping out onto the small deck, Jax put aside her enjoyment at being so close to the clapping sea waters and turned her attention to the side of the boat. Leaning against the rail without thinking of her own safety, she craned her neck toward the large window she'd seen from inside Lady Florence's cabin. Standing on the tips of her toes, she teetered dangerously forward, her attention diverted to the silent sea below.

"Are you mad?" Perry exclaimed as he rushed outside to join

her, clasping her flailing arms as she scanned the side of the *Rose* for any hint as to what might have happened.

"I'm fine," Jax said as she batted him off, setting her two feet firmly on the deck of the balcony. "Her curtains are drawn now, but they weren't yesterday when Uma, Hendrie, and I looked around. Grandeair very well could have seen something, maybe even unknowingly, and the criminal, fearing capture, killed him."

"All for a piece of jewelry?" Perry asked with dubious eyes.

Jax gave him a severe look. "People have been killed for far less, Lord Pettraud."

"The man was also a moneylender. Perhaps someone from his business dealings came back to haunt him."

"You'd think if that was the case, we would have spotted recognition or resentment of him by someone on board. He appeared to not know any of the guests before this voyage. Even if he doesn't meet his debtors in person, he would still know them by name." Jax stepped gingerly back into the cabin with the dead man and approached the small desk in the corner of the room. "But you could be right. With the man being a moneylender, perhaps this was someone's way of paying their debt. Maybe a member of the crew did this? I've hardly seen any of them since we've boarded. It's almost as if they are invisible," she stated, more to herself than to Perry. Gently, she pried open the top drawer, discovering a leather-bound journal resting peacefully on top of a stack of documents. Her fingers nimbly unwound the leather cord around the cover, flipping through the myriad of pages, each filled with extensive, scrawling writing. "If that's the case, here is our list of suspects." She held up the journal so Perry could see it. "This is a record of all the loans and payments the man has arranged over the years. Some of these people have been paying him back for decades," she paused, reading through the record of someone named *F. Voltistè*, "at an exorbitant amount of interest."

"Do any of the names match our companions?" Perry came to her side, peering at the book.

She quickly scanned the last fifty pages or so, with nothing jumping out at her. "I'll take this back to my room and take a closer look."

"Absolutely not," Perry growled, ripping the ledger from her hand. "This might be the only evidence we have. What if the killer comes back here and discovers it missing? If he or she finds out you took it, I shudder to think what would happen."

"But Perry, they could destroy it, then what will we have to go on?" Jax cried out, incredulous that he wanted to leave something so valuable behind.

"I know, which is why *I'm* going to take it and make sure everyone knows it's in my possession, not yours." He looked at her, his features softening.

She blushed, the intense gaze of his affection making her feel a bit lightheaded. "You're one of a kind, Lord Pettraud," she whispered, feeling it inappropriate to say anything more passionate in the presence of a dead man. "Now, we must speak to the guards and alert Carriena before someone else stumbles into this mess."

The tender moment between them broken by the unfortunate reality of the situation, Perry nodded and ushered Jax out of the room, closing the door with a snap. She charged ahead, rushing down the long passage to the doorframe where Diego and Ferdinand stood, their expressions telling her they sensed something was wrong.

"Is Monsieur Grandeair all right, Duchess?" Diego asked. "You were with him for quite some time."

Taking a deep breath, Jax shook her head. "I'm afraid not, Diego. Please, can you tell me if you noticed anyone enter the banker's room last night during your shift?"

Both young men appeared startled by her sudden change in topic. Ferdinand cleared his throat and spoke first. "We arrived here at three in the morning, Your Grace. No one opened a door until breakfast."

When Diego nodded in agreement, Jax's shoulder's sagged. "I guess I'll have to wake up poor Sebastián and Eduardo again," she said with a sigh before launching into a quiet explanation for her questions. She chose her words carefully, only telling the two guards that Monsieur Grandeair had passed away during the night and they were not to go in the room nor let anyone else enter without permission directly from Carriena or herself. Both guards' youthful ages showed in their sickened expressions as she concluded her story. She doubted either of them had the courage to disobey her direct orders, despite her not being their captain or ducal leader.

Leaving the lads to stand watch over the ominously dark corridor, Jax and Perry rushed onto the main deck, grateful to fill their lungs with clean air. Despite her familiarity with it, the smell of death still unsettled Jax immensely.

"Perry, gather George and Carriena together and fill them in on what we have learned so far," Jax delegated with authority. "I'm going down to speak with Eduardo and Sebastián. They must have seen someone go into the man's room last night."

Perry gave her a dubious look. "I don't think it's safe for you to be alone, Jax."

She was about to protest when she spotted Hendrie emerging from the dining hall door. "Well, I won't be. I'll take Hendrie down with me," she said with a triumphant huff, gesturing the valet over to her side.

The straw-haired young man seemed nervous, obviously sensing the tension between the two royals. "Down where, Your Grace?" he asked.

"I'll fill you in once we are inside, Hendrie, but we need to get downstairs to speak with the evening guards." Without another word of explanation, Jax took off, leaving Perry miffed in her wake.

Knocking on the sentries' cabin door moments later, Jax could hardly contain the anxiety building up in her chest. She'd noticed the slack sails when she'd been up on deck, and the thought of floating in the middle of the sea with a murderer aboard heightened her desperation to get off this ship. Hendrie was wise enough to keep silent as he stood patiently by her side, but she could sense fear radiating from him.

This time Sebastián was the one to open the door, his face registering surprise at the sight of the Duchess in the hallway once again. "Your Grace? Has there been another theft?"

If only. "I'm afraid it's something more serious this time, Sebastián. Monsieur Grandeair passed away sometime during the night."

The guard's jaw dropped in astonishment. "Virtues, no! That's terrible news. I hope he didn't suffer; he looked downright rancid when he came back to his room last night. Eduardo offered to escort him down the hall, but he just batted us away. We thought it was only seasickness affecting him. Goodness, I feel terrible."

Jax listened intently, but felt obligated to correct the poor boy to alleviate his guilt. "He didn't die from seasickness, Sebastián. But I must ask, did you notice anyone enter his room after he returned last night?"

Any relief Sebastián felt was overcome with confusion and deep thought. "What? Well, let me think about it." Seconds ticked by as he pondered the question. "No, I don't believe anyone did. Grandeair returned by himself and went into his room. Then, about a half hour later, the other guests all came back together. Everyone was in good spirits, talking about Lady Giovanna's performance. Lady Florence, who'd come back much earlier in the evening, came out from her cabin and started asking everyone to forgive her wretched behavior. Of course, everyone accepted her apology, and they all had a bit of a laugh about it. Then, everyone disappeared into their rooms for the night, and not a single door opened for the rest of our shift."

By this time, a bleary-eyed Eduardo arrived at the door, bowing his head when he saw the Duchess. "I didn't expect to see you back so soon, Your Grace." He smiled.

"A guest has died, Ed," Sebastián said, his voice somber. "Why don't you tell the Duchess what happened last night in your own words?"

Jax realized that Sebastián appeared to be the sharpest of the guards she'd spoken with thus far. He knew that by having Eduardo share his version of the story, when and if they aligned, she'd know the young guards were speaking the truth.

Eduardo did indeed share the previous night's events, his account mirroring Sebastián's own words, but with a more dramatic flair. Specifically, how Eduardo had overheard Charles reprimand his sister for flirting with the Master Builder. While not exactly incriminating, Jax mentally filed it away for later consideration.

"Thank you, gentlemen, for your time. Once again, I apologize for interrupting your sleep," she said, trying to mask her disappointment at how little she had learned.

Once they were out of earshot from the closed door, Hendrie whispered, "I take it from your line of questioning that Monsieur Grandeair did not peacefully pass away in the nighttime."

Pulling Hendrie along the passageway, she only stopped when they were in the stairwell, her eyes watching for any movement around them. "I'm afraid you're right," she confirmed in a whisper. "The poor man was stabbed several times in the back. Perry and I found him before anyone else did."

Hendrie visibly swallowed. "Well, if our guards are to be believed, no one entered his room after he returned from the ballroom. Just like the brooch that was stolen from Lady Florence." The valet suddenly looked ashen. "Please tell me there's not a vengeful ghost aboard this ship."

Jax rolled her eyes at his childish fear. "Virtues, no, Hendrie, be reasonable," she chastised, while simultaneously acknowledging that he did bring up a good point. How had someone been able to enter Grandeair's room and kill him without being seen by the guards? She thought back to the small, yet well-decorated cabin. "Of course! The balcony!" Jax hissed. "Grandeair's room has a balcony attached, looking out over the ocean. Yesterday, Diego said that someone could, in theory, drop down from the top deck onto a balcony as another point of entry into the lower deck cabins. I dismissed it at the time, because Lady Florence's room did not have a terrace, so her brooch couldn't have been stolen by those means."

Hendrie looked unconvinced. "You think someone on board this ship lowered themselves from the top deck all the way onto the dead man's balcony? That's got to be a fifteen-foot drop at the least."

"It's possible they landed on the balcony attached to Carriena's suite first. Her rooms are directly above that of Monsieur Grandeair." Jax stroked her chin thoughtfully. "It certainly would take a great deal of physical strength to do so, which limits our suspects greatly. I can't imagine someone of Ernest Haulsinger's bulk dangling over the side of the *Rose*."

The valet did not laugh at her light jab. Instead, he met her gaze with a worried grimace. "Please don't hate me for suggesting this, but it could be possible that the culprit started out on the terrace of Lady Carriena's suite and climbed down onto Grandeair's balcony."

Jax knew immediately what Hendrie was implying, and although she didn't agree with him in the slightest, she acknowledged his words with respect. "While it is in the realm of possibility that Carriena *could* have done such a thing, I do not think it probable. What does she have to gain from this man's death? Only trouble and turmoil for her duchy."

"I understand your allegiance to her, Your Grace. I just meant that we need to consider all options objectively."

Hendrie appeared to tremble under her stare. Jax felt a swell of admiration for the young man, as well as a twist of burning heartache. While being wise enough not to voice his full thoughts, Jax knew what the valet was ultimately getting at. She had to consider that her emotions and attachments to people had clouded her judgment in the past, and it had led to deadly results. "You are quite right, Hendrie." She felt a lump forming in her throat. "We do need to investigate all avenues, regardless of personal opinions." Her cheeks burned with shame, both with the regrets of the past, and knowing that she was betraying a valued friendship by even considering the possibility that Carriena could be guilty. But Hendrie did have a point. Her suite was right above Grandeair's...

"Jax! There you are," Perry called from the top of the staircase, his unruly curls plastered to his forehead with sweat. "Carriena has been looking for you. She and Hazel are about to," he lowered his voice, "visit Grandeair."

Jax felt her stomach clench. "Hazel?"

Perry nodded. "Carriena demanded Monsieur Grandeair be examined, but she sided with your suggestion of keeping it secret for now. Hazel will be asked to take some oath of the Ancient Faith that binds her to secrecy. Apparently, Carriena learned of it during her studies at the Academy."

Jax recalled that Carriena had taken a special elective course in the Ancient Faith, considering Isla DeLacqua had a large population of its followers living amongst its watery borders. Jax had opted to take a class called The Art of Persuasion during that term. "And are we certain this is an oath Hazel won't break?"

Perry looked at her grimly. "Apparently, if she does break it, the gods of the Ancient Faith will burn her family alive. So, yes, we are as certain as we can be in this situation."

Jax heaved her shoulders with a hint of defeat. "So be it. Let's go." As they made their way up from the service quarters, Jax and Hendrie filled Perry in on what little they had learned from the guards, as well as their speculations regarding the murderer entering from Grandeair's balcony. At the entrance of the lower deck, Hendrie departed to find Uma and the other guests, while Perry and Jax continued down the long hallway where Captain Solomon stood guard at the deceased banker's door.

"Lady Carriena and the High Priestess are inside. Hazel has already pledged her oath of secrecy," George reported, opening the door for Jax to enter. She tried to squash her disappointment that she hadn't been present herself to hear it. Hendrie's veiled accusation gnawed away at her, her thoughts being twisted against her friend. Had George actually heard the oath? What if Carriena and Hazel were in on this together? Pushing her poisonous thoughts aside, she walked calmly into the dark room, the growing smell of blood and decay assaulting her nose.

Chapter Seven

"Oh, Jax, thank goodness you're here," Carriena blurted out, forgetting to use the Duchess's full name in front of a relative stranger. The young woman looked sick to her stomach, her skin barely reflecting any color. Was guilt getting the better of her?

Jax chided herself inwardly, trying to shake away the unsettling thoughts. "I'm sorry it took me so long, my dear friend. I was speaking with the guards to try and figure out what may have happened."

"What have they got to say for themselves? How could they let this happen on their watch?" Carriena nearly shrieked.

Jax lay a calming arm on her friend's shoulder. "Neither shift saw anything unusual in the hallway. I'm afraid we've got quite the mastermind on board."

"Oh Virtues, help us! We're stranded in the middle of the sea with a killer." Carriena wept openly into her hands, her shoulders shaking uncontrollably.

Jax was well aware of Hazel's stoic presence, the High Priestess's face almost bored in its expression. "Priestess, have you looked at the wounds?"

"Only superficially, Your Grace, but now that you are here, I will examine them closer." With fluid grace, Hazel knelt at the dead man's side, gingerly pulling off the bloodstained dress shirt, revealing a pimple-pocked, flabby back. With the tunic removed, Jax could plainly see that the man had been stabbed five or six times.

Hazel studied the body in silence for a few, tense moments, Carriena's muffled weeping the only sound in the room. "I believe this to be the first blow, here." The High Priestess pointed to a gash just beneath the man's left shoulder blade. "It also killed him rather instantly. It severed something near his heart. Without cutting him open, I won't be able to tell exactly what the blade nicked, but you can see that this wound had the most blood protrude from it, and the other wounds are shallower and less gory. The heart had already stopped pumping blood by the time they were made," Hazel surmised with an unnerving calm that Jax rather admired.

"A blade you say? Do you know what type of weapon did this?" Jax asked in a hushed tone.

Hazel frowned, apparently unsure. "The wounds have morphed a bit, as the body has started to stiffen, but I'd say something akin to a dinner knife. Certainly nothing large, like a sword or dagger."

"A dinner knife? We've all had access to more than one over the past three days," Carriena sobbed, helpless in her grief.

Jax buried her annoyance at the woman's hysterics. "Hazel, is it possible to tell how long he has been dead?"

"Judging by the rigor in his limbs, I'd say the poor soul has been like this since well before dawn. It's not much to go on, I'm afraid." Her dark skin glowed in the candlelight flickering from the wall, casting shadows on her grim expression.

"Well, at least that narrows down that he was killed well before everyone left their rooms for breakfast," Jax said as she folded her arms, thinking with renewed determination. "Carriena, I think it would be wise to send Captain Solomon down to the service quarters and thoroughly question all of the ship's crew. Although it's been reported that no one entered or left this room at any point in the night, perhaps they saw or heard something downstairs that could be of use."

Carriena nodded blindly, wiping her eyes free of the torrent of tears. "Of course. Yes, right away. Goodness, I can't believe that while I slept, a man was being murdered right below me."

Jax squeezed her friend's hand in sympathy, the action suddenly bringing a memory from last night to the forefront of her troubled mind. She had urged Carriena to retire early for the evening, and the young woman had obliged without question, not even staying long enough to hear Lady Giovanna perform a single song. Carriena, who had been a terror at the Academy, always staying up late, hosting the wildest of gatherings, had simply gone to bed without any protest, even at the prospect of a performance by a renowned bard. The unsettling realization haunted her footsteps as she left and walked into the hallway, where George and Perry stood waiting.

"George, I need you to go down to the service quarters and question everyone about last night and their whereabouts," Jax instructed. "I'm particularly curious if anyone in the bunks beneath Monsieur Grandeair's room heard anything suspicious. It appears the man was stabbed six times in the back, but Virtues have mercy, he died quickly after the first. Hazel seems to think the weapon was the size of a dinner knife, although the hardening of the body after death could have changed the size of the wounds," she explained with a calmness she did not feel.

"I'll keep my eyes open for such a weapon while I am downstairs. Do you want me to report to you and Carriena after I've concluded my interviews?" George asked.

Jax gave him a hard look. "No, only me. I'll explain to you later, but we would be wise to consider everyone on this ship a suspect," she warned, her voice low and barely audible.

She watched as George and Perry exchanged a surprised look, but they did not inquire further. George simply bowed and headed down into the belly of the ship.

Taking Jax by the arm, Perry briskly led her away from Monsieur Grandeair's door and up the stairs to the main deck. "Mind telling me what that was all about? You are seriously considering Carriena to be behind all of this?"

Storming up to the bow of the ship, Jax seethed at the doubt lacing his words. "Yes, I am seriously considering it. It wouldn't be the first time a childhood friend of mine has turned out to be a coldblooded killer," she spat back at him, although unable to meet his gaze.

Instead of a heated reply, she felt a warm hand cradle her elbow, pulling her back into the safety of his chest. He didn't chastise her, or tell her she was being senseless; he simply held her tightly until the flourishing pain in her chest subsided and she trusted herself to speak the words in her heart. "I know it's cruel for me to think so poorly of her, Perry, but I'm just so afraid that I'm right."

"I know, my love. I know." His arms gripped her more fiercely.

At his words, she pulled back, staring up into his beautifully sincere eyes. "Really? You do?"

A tender smile graced his lips. "Yes, I do. I know how you are feeling, and I love you for it. You're such a strong woman, Jax. That, I know. I love that you can be vulnerable with me." He gave her a delicate kiss on the forehead, all her worries and concerns vanishing for the moment.

"You and no other, Perry." She buried her face in his shoulder, tears of relief cascading down her cheekbones. "I love you, too, Lord Pettraud. If I am sure about anything in all this madness, it's that."

Chapter Eight

They were interrupted a few moments later by the appearance of Charles, a book in his hand. "Greetings, Duchess. Quite the series of events that's happened today, and it's not even lunchtime." The young man grinned with boyish exuberance.

The jovial scene in the dining hall seemed like ages ago, but Jax realized it was not yet midday. "Have I missed any stimulating discussions, Sir Charles? I've had a busy morning myself."

"Besides the announcement of poor Monsieur Grandeair's passing?" Tucking the book under his arm, Charles motioned to the sweeping sea all around them. "Well, it seems as though the Sea of Intelligence has plans to keep us all together for longer than we expected."

Taken aback by the young scholar's nonchalant mood concerning the banker's death, Jax glimpsed up at the limp sails. "I hope no one is troubled by that."

Charles laughed rather flippantly. "I certainly am in no rush to arrive in Isla DeLacqua. I'm perfectly content holding off on my training and onto my freedom for as long as possible."

Jax frowned at the Hestian's sudden difference in tune. "When we last spoke of your physician residency, you were excited about it. Has something changed?"

Charles walked to the railing, leaning against it, and looking out into the distance. "I guess it finally dawned on me that I'll be alone in Isla DeLacqua for who knows how long. My sister doesn't plan to stay more than a fortnight before returning home to our father and mother. And when she does, it will be just me," he shared, a sweet, innocent sadness radiating from him. Turning back to face Perry and Jax, he continued, "I've always looked after my little sister, you know. I'm the one who's kept her safe in the circles she runs in. You know the reputations bards and actors have. I'm afraid she'll go astray without me being there to protect her."

Beside her, Jax felt Perry bristle. She wondered for a moment if any of his older brothers cared for him as fiercely as Charles did for his sister. "I'm sure Lady Giovanna will be just fine. You've set a good example for her, but you must allow her to live her own life, as well as live your own to the fullest," Jax advised with wisdom she hoped did not sound false.

In response, Charles bowed low. "You are the great ruler the realm proclaims you to be, Duchess." He backed away from the couple, giving them their privacy on the main deck once more.

Perry chuckled as Charles disappeared.

"What's so funny?" Jax asked.

"An overprotective brother at his finest. Obviously, the poor lad is worried that his sister is falling for our resident master builder," Perry said with mock slyness.

She gave a dismissive shrug. "Well, she's an adult woman, she can fall in love with whoever she wants."

"Eh, I'd be worried, too, if my one and only sister was being swept off her feet by that skirt-chaser."

"Perry!" Jax was astounded at his use of such a lewd term. "How dare you?" She couldn't suppress a fit of giggles, feeling a bit guilty after the morning's events. "What on earth makes you say that?"

"I guess you can't always catch everything, even when it's right in front of your eyes, Duchess," Perry teased. "That man has tried to corner every woman at some point during this trip. Poor Uma was fighting him off the first night at dinner, and Hazel didn't give him the time of day. Goodness, he even was flirting with Lady Florence as he escorted her to breakfast this morning. I could practically hear it from clear across the ship! At least the cad had the sense not to go anywhere near you." Perry smirked, leaving Jax to wonder what her suitor's reaction would have been had the craftsman tried to seduce her.

"Maybe I should have a talk with Lady Giovanna, just to make sure she knows what she's getting into." Jax's eyes followed the stairs from the bow leading down to the rest of the main deck. "I'll go see if I can find her now."

Giving Perry a secretive kiss on the cheek, Jax scanned the boat, looking for any sign of the singer. Vincent and Ernest were playing cards, Archer was once again reading, and Hazel and Lady Florence were sitting in chairs, drinking tea. No one seemed the least bit affected by the news of Grandeair's passing.

"You look like you are in search of something, Duchess," Vincent's smooth voice beckoned her over to the card table. "May we be of assistance?"

"I was hoping to speak with Lady Giovanna. Have you seen her?" she asked, looking between the two contrasting men, as different in appearance as the moon and sun.

Vincent sat back in his chair, his long, sinewy limbs gleaming under his ebony skin. "I thought I saw her disappear below deck a little while ago. Perhaps she is still there?" He cleared his throat as she turned to leave, indicating he was not done speaking. "I know your consort was asking my Hazel if she carried any cloveroot on her person. For his painting?" His words were spoken with a slow, lilted drawl.

Jax froze for a moment before finding the right response. "Yes, Lord Pettraud is extremely talented with a brush. I know he had been hoping to paint the sea while we sailed."

Vincent nodded, pulling his hand of cards close to his rippling chest. "While he won't find any on Isla DeLacqua, I know there is a reputable cloveroot farm in Beautraud. Perhaps you can stop by on your return to Saphire so he may replenish his stock?"

Caught in a dangerous lie, it amazed Jax that grumpy old Ernest unknowingly came to her rescue. "Bah, don't bother going through Beautraud. That duchy has fallen into shambles in recent years. We traveled through it on our way from Savant, and it was a nightmare. Never have I tasted such horrible food than at the inns we stayed in."

Jax grimaced, backing away from the card table. "Thank you both for your unsolicited advice. I'll leave you to return to your game," she said curtly, and resumed searching the deck once more for Giovanna's slim figure.

While she was disappointed not to find the young singer, another absence troubled her more. Where was Carriena? Jax hadn't paid close enough attention to her friend's movements after the examination of the body. Was she still downstairs in Grandeair's cabin? Could she be searching for the ledger Perry now had hidden away in his rooms?

Hoisting her skirts, Jax hurried at an unladylike pace toward the lower deck. Muttering a faint greeting as she barged past Ferdinand and Diego, Jax rushed down the long corridor, the dim candlelight creating an eerie path. Passing by cabins two and four, Jax halted, hearing a door open ahead of her. Looking around, and realizing there was nowhere to hide, she wondered how she could explain being on the lower deck when her suite was upstairs.

She saw a slender figure emerge from what appeared to be cabin eight. Thinking back to the manifest, Jax remembered it being the room assigned to Archer. Embarrassed for the encounter that was about to occur, Jax smoothed her skirts and walked casually down the hallway, feigning disbelief at running into Lady Giovanna.

"Duchess! What a surprise to see you down here," the singer trilled. "Are you looking for someone? Last I checked, we were all up on the main deck, getting some sun." She didn't appear at all put off by the Duchess's presence.

Jax was astonished that Giovanna showed no shame at being caught leaving Archer's room. She had thought highly of the young lady, but now, wasn't so sure of her innocent nature. "Yes, um, I was hoping to speak with your brother about his plans after his residency concludes. I have a few towns in Saphire that require a skilled physician." The lie rolled off Jax's lips with feigned finesse, but she had to cross her hands behind her back to keep from wringing them.

"Oh, he's upstairs reading on the main deck. I was just grabbing a book from his room myself." Giggling, Lady Giovanna held up a worn novel in her ageless hands. "He always packs much better than I do. Silly me, thinking my companions would be up for constantly entertaining me. My brother is a bit superstitious and is afraid to come down here, with a dead body and all, so I had to come fetch a book myself." She hunched her shoulders. "You'd think an apprenticing physician would be used to death by now, but who am I to judge?"

"You were coming out of your brother's room?" Jax asked, realizing as soon as the words were out of her mouth how crass she sounded.

"Yes, of course. Where else would I be coming from, Your Grace?" Giovanna's question was poised with the innocence and naiveté reflective of her youth.

"Goodness me, I'm not sure. The dim light down here is playing tricks with my eyes, I suppose." Jax forced a flippant laugh. She ushered Giovanna down the hall toward the stairs. "Please, don't mind me. I guess I've been standing in the sun too long."

The young actress studied Jax for a scrutinizing moment before backing away and going up the stairs to the main deck. Jax watched after her, her embarrassment beginning to simmer down. Turning her attention down the long passage, she put to bed her mistake, convincing herself that the flickering candlelight and seemingly endless walls played tricks on her eyes. She resumed her march toward the far room belonging to Monsieur Grandeair, reaching out to grasp the handle with a tentative hand. She was discouraged, yet not completely surprised, to find it locked.

Examining the brass door in search of her next move, Jax reached up into her hair, plucking a pin from her honeyed tresses. Not wanting to explain why she wanted access to Grandeair's room to the guards in exchange for the master key, Jax tried her luck at lock picking, listening with care to the inner workings of the contraption. She remembered her days at the Academy, using these deviously acquired skills to unlock forbidden rooms or a professor's desk, Carriena and Arnie always standing watch to alert her of unwanted company. In those days, she thought their friendship would never falter, no matter what hand life dealt each of them. Her heart restricted in her chest as she thought about how far gone those days were.

Her stomach seized as the mechanism in the lock lurched into place, a noticeable click revealing her success. What good was a locked door if a flimsy hairpin was enough to sabotage it? How secure were they on this ship? Had these doors been intentionally designed like this? Unnerving questions boiled to the surface of her mind, and Jax noted she would approach Captain Valhalen about this once he was back on his feet.

Pushing open the cabin door, Jax dashed into the room, closing it behind her. She was startled by the haunting shape of a body lying underneath a white sheet, Monsieur Grandeair resting peacefully on the bare mattress of the bed. She guessed he would remain here for the rest of the voyage, as Master Archer had likely not built a tomb for the ship's guests. She looked around the lifeless space, wondering what she had hoped to learn here. Had she really expected Carriena to still be standing over the body, laughing at her victory? Shuddering, Jax took a timid step toward the dead man's figure, reaching a shaking hand out and lifting back the white sheet.

Whomever had arranged the body like this had done so with care. A new shirt had been put on Grandeair, and the dried blood had been wiped from his mouth. His eyes were closed and his features poised so that he appeared to be fast asleep. It was startling how normal he looked, despite being dead for hours. Summoning her courage and her strong stomach, Jax grasped the man's shoulders, hauling him up to his side. She wanted to assess the wounds for herself, no longer trusting the relationship between Carriena and Hazel. If the High Priestess was colluding with her friend, perhaps she had given Jax misinformation regarding the type of weapon used to end the man's life.

Monsieur Grandeair's back was ghastly pale, blue and green veins nearly bulging up under the pasty skin. Gasping back her nausea, Jax studied the gashes, her amethyst eyes begging for answers. The lacerations were indeed small; a large blade could not have struck and torn so little skin. Jax counted the six blemishes across the man's back, astonished by the viciousness needed to commit such a personal and intimate act. Her eyes landed last on the wound just beneath the left shoulder blade, the one that Hazel said had ended Grandeair's life, and therefore, the one that had bled out the most. She leaned as close as she dared to, examining the gash, narrowing in on the damaged skin around it. She could almost see the faint trace of a bruise, in the odd shape of a starburst. Jax remembered where she'd seen something like that before. It was a well-known injury in jousting, often resulting in the death of knight bearing it. She and her father would visit the infirmary after a duel to pay their respects to injured or fallen knights. Master Vyanti had explained to her once that the knights could be bruised by the hilt of the blade that ran them through; the Ancient Faith considered it to be a mark of death. At the time, Jax had rolled her eyes at the archaic religion's beliefs. It would be impossible to escape death after being run through with a sword, all the way up to the hilt; of course, the imprint of the grip would foreshadow demise. But she had learned one valuable thing during those trips— the bruise of the hilt was nearly a perfect silhouette of the top of the weapon's handle. Looking down at Grandeair's back, Jax knew that the murder weapon would have a starburst shape where the hilt and blade forged together. Something so unique surely would be easy for her to track down.

Laying the body back as it was and pulling the sheet over it once more, Jax backed away from the corpse, rushing to the basin to scrub her hands free of death. As she plunged her hands repeatedly into the porcelain bowl of water, the starburst pattern circled foremost in her mind. Once she dried her hands on her skirts, she quietly dipped out into the hallway, debating where to look first. Hazel had said the weapon could have been a dinner knife, so she decided to check the galley for any evidence.

‡

The kitchen staff scrambled to tidy themselves up at the presence of the Duchess as she walked fluidly into the room, which steamed with heat despite the windows being open. Jax guessed the stagnant sea breeze affected the circulation of air in the belly of the ship as well as the sails.

A tall, mustached man in a stained apron approached her curiously, his beady eyes blinking back the sweat stemming from underneath the rim of his chef's hat. "Greetings, Your Grace. May we assist you with something?"

Jax realized she was speaking to the famed Monsieur Devoyier, a Savant commoner who had cooked for the nation's ducal table. "Is that our luncheon I see bubbling? It smells divine," she said, taking a moment to appreciate the glorious aromas wafting around her. "I do have a request. It may sound a bit odd, but I'd like to look at the silverware the guests have been using." Jax paused, searching for an excuse. "I'm considering redesigning one of my retreats in Saphire, and I'd like to see if I can get any inspiration for the banquet room."

If he thought her explanation odd, Monsieur Devoyier masked it with precision. "Of course, Duquessa. Please, right this way," he said, leading her into a side room containing two huge cabinets. "The linens for the table are in this drawer," the chef said, motioning accordingly, "and the dining sets are in the two top ones." He bowed with a flourish and left Jax to examine her options.

Pulling open the first compartment underneath the glass case showing stacks of golden rimmed plates, Jax scanned the contents. She counted four styles of dinnerware, each set containing thirty-three forks, spoons, and knives. Jax guessed that was the seating capacity of the long, gleaming dining table. None of the knives appeared to have a handle matching the starburst imprint she'd found on the murdered man's back.

Closing the drawer with a disappointed thud, she heaved out the one directly below it. This compartment was crammed full of shining metals, Jax counting six assorted styles. Her eyes settled on the set lying farthest to the right, displaying handles that were molded into the shape of an eight-pointed star where the blade merged with the grip. Picking one up to examine it closer, Jax immediately knew as she looked down the length of the short blade that the bruising around the banker's wound mirrored the sight in front of her now. A rush of excitement thundered through her veins as Jax leaned in to count the knives in the starburst set. Thirty-two rested in the drawer. One was indeed missing. *It had to be the murder weapon!* "Excuse me," she called back into the kitchen. When one of the ship's pursers rushed over to her side, she asked, "Have we used this particular set thus far during the voyage?"

"Not in the formal dining room, Your Grace," the young man answered without pause. "However, we did serve a light lunch to the guests who arrived before we set sail from Tandora. I believe this was the set we used."

Jax felt her pulse quicken. "Do you happen to remember who attended that luncheon, by any chance?"

The assistant clicked his tongue, trying to bring forth the memory. "I believe it was nearly all of Lady Carriena's guests, save the Saphire party, as Your Grace did not arrive until later in the afternoon."

Her enthusiasm dimmed at this news. The man was telling her what she already knew; that all the other passengers were still suspect. Nevertheless, she thanked him for the information and left the galley in search of Perry and George to share what she had learned. As she ascended the stairs to the main deck, she prayed to the Virtues that George had uncovered something while speaking to the ship's crew. Otherwise, she was afraid all her leads were taking them toward a dismal dead end.

Chapter Nine

"No one saw or heard anything? How is that possible?" Jax cried in frustration, flinging her arms up in the air as she paced around her suite. "Do you think they were telling the truth?" She turned, facing the Captain of the Ducal Guard.

"Yes, I do," George replied from his perch on one of the sitting room chairs. "This boat is built with sturdy, dense wood. The walls are thick. I'm inclined to believe they wouldn't have heard anything, especially if the crew was asleep. They are working incredibly hard to keep the passengers happy and the ship looking regal and refined. No doubt they are all exhausted by the time they're back in their rooms."

"Hendrie and I agree," Uma said. "We've heard them complaining, for lack of a better word, when we've been down in the kitchen filling up the water buckets. They may be tired and overworked, but the crew and staff have been so kind to us. I hardly think any of them are capable of murder, or even stealing. Besides," she added, "the guards saw no one enter or leave the passageway. How could anyone from the service quarters sneak past two alert guards twice without them noticing?"

Jax thought back briefly to her miscalculation of Lady Giovanna leaving Charles's room. But even then, she'd still seen the young woman in the hallway. Uma was right; there was no way for someone to sneak past. "Then that leaves us with someone entering Grandeair's room from the balcony."

Perry leaned forward in the chair he was sitting in. "Jax, I know it pains you to think about it, but would Carriena have anything to gain by murdering a banker?"

Jax crossed her arms, her forehead wrinkling with deep thought. "Her father was bringing Monsieur Grandeair to their duchy to review the treasury. The Duke has been concerned with the nation's finances. Why would Carriena want to stop that?"

Hendrie cleared his throat from the corner. "Perhaps Lady Carriena is the reason behind the treasury's issues?"

"You think she could be stealing from her own duchy?" George looked shocked by the notion.

Jax, too, felt like the wind had been knocked out of her. "I can't see a reason why she would feel the need to steal. It makes no sense."

"Perhaps she was funneling the money to someone else?" Perry suggested, putting his hands together as he reasoned out a motive.

"Let's for a moment assume that Carriena was not involved with this. For Virtues' sake, her birthday is tomorrow!" Jax pointed out to the assembled group. "Who on board could have dropped down from the top deck onto Grandeair's balcony?"

"Don't forget, this person would also have had to have climbed back up to the top deck to escape detection. Then there's the whole issue of how they got back into their own rooms," George said, his dark eyes reminding Jax of all the contributing factors, his logic unwavering.

"All right, then. Let's see. First, who is physically able to accomplish such a feat?" Jax questioned aloud, thinking of the guests she'd met over the past few days.

"Master Archer, for one. And he has intimate knowledge of the layout of the boat," Uma offered.

"Both Vincent and Hazel are strong and lithe. I'm sure neither would have any trouble making the climb," Perry said.

"I haven't seen Hazel wear anything suitable for climbing," Jax countered.

Perry shrugged. "Perhaps she wore a pair of Vincent's trousers?"

"I'd wager a guess that Charles could do it, and being a

physician, he'd know exactly where to stab someone to ensure they bled to death quickly." George scratched his growing beard, as if imaging the lanky young man wielding a deadly weapon.

"All right, now which one those four has a room with a balcony of its own? They would have needed to climb out from their room, up to the main deck, then drop themselves down onto Grandeair's landing." As Jax voiced the theory, she realized how silly it all sounded. She was making her friends exert their sharp minds on a scenario that was nearly impossible.

She could tell from the blank faces in the room that they knew it was fruitless, but humored her anyway.

"I reviewed drawings of the ship's layout earlier today with Felipe and Alonso, the guards who watch the upper deck staterooms during the night," George reported. "Rooms five, six, nine, and ten are all equipped with balconies of various sizes."

"Grandeair is in cabin nine," Jax said. She thought back to the dimly lit image of the passenger manifest Diego had held in his hands the other day. "Giovanna is in cabin five, Hazel is across from her in cabin six, and Charles is in ten."

"Based on our physical assessment, that narrows it down to Hazel or Charles," Perry said grimly.

"Both have intimate knowledge of the human anatomy, which means they would know where to strike their victim," Jax murmured, thinking back to how Hazel interacted with the dead body. "But if that's the case, why would they have stabbed Grandeair five more times if they knew the first blow would have killed him?"

Uma wrung her hands together, coming to Jax's side. "Maybe their passion and bloodlust momentarily overrode reason?"

Jax nodded, understanding her lady's maid's words, but she did not agree. The thought that young, naïve Charles or serene, religious Hazel was a killer was almost more farfetched than Carriena committing the crime. Then there was the question of where the theft of Lady Florence's brooch and the poisoning of Captain Valhalen fit in. "I'm at a loss, I'm afraid," Jax sighed, her shoulders sagging under the immense pressure. "We must be missing something." She suddenly looked over to Perry. "Have you found anything of use in Grandeair's ledger?"

Any hope she had crumbled when Perry shook his head of chaotic dark curls. "Nothing. Not a single name rings any bells. If it did, we'd have our killer. The amount that man forced people to pay him in return was murder itself. Truth be told, I'm surprised he lived as long as he did," Perry said, a bleak chuckle dying on his lips.

Jax ran a hand through her hair, getting a fingernail caught in a ringlet. "All right, well, since I'm absolutely useless, I suggest we all return to our rooms and prepare for dinner. I'm famished; I'm sorry I forced you all to miss lunch for this pointless session." The Duchess dismissed her companions, going over to her window overlooking the silent sea. The wind was as elusive as the truth.

"Jax," Perry said, his hand touching her shoulder, "you're not absolutely useless. You're putting too much pressure on yourself to get to the bottom of this. You're a Duchess, remember. No one expects you to solve every puzzle that comes your way." His lavender eyes pooled with sincerity.

His words hurt her deeply, as much as she hated to admit it. He didn't believe that she could figure this out, that the mystery was too great for her pretty little mind. She knew he had meant to comfort her, but she pushed him away, her pride sore. "I'd like some time alone with my thoughts, Lord Pettraud, if you please." She extended her hand sharply toward the door.

Perry's eyes crinkled with unmasked sadness as he backed away. "As you command, Duchess," he said with a curt bow, leaving the room silent in his wake.

Uma stood awkwardly by the washroom door, unsure it was her place to speak. "Shall I fill the bath for you, my lady?" she asked with a halting shyness Jax remembered from their early days together.

Putting a palm against her forehead to simmer her frustrations, Jax nodded, fearing she would snap if she spoke. She'd hurt Perry intentionally, and now Uma was tiptoeing around her like they weren't close companions. It was as if this voyage was determined to drive her mad.

✝

Dressed in a pale green silk gown, her golden crown jewels resting on her plaited hair, Jax glided into the dining hall for the evening's meal. Everyone was already engaged in conversation, as Jax had taken a brief detour on her way from her suite. She had stood on the ship's bow, looking up the stars, the night sky an endless canopy of twinkling light. The lavender-scented bath water had done her good, and the majestic sky had helped empty and refocus her mind. Walking into the banquet hall now, she took a moment to walk next to Perry and squeeze his shoulder before going to her seat. She hoped she conveyed her regrets in the simple gesture, and the impishly charming look on his face told her she had as she sat down across from him.

"Tonight, we raise a glass to our dearly departed Monsieur Grandeair," Carriena lamented. "May the Virtues take care of his soul." She raised a goblet in the shadows of the chandelier.

"To Grandeair!" A chorus of mournful voices responded, each guest taking a long drink of their mead. Jax and her party all waited until everyone else had swallowed before pulling the drink through their lips.

As if a flame had burst into existence, everyone's mood suddenly shifted into a more jovial atmosphere. Jogan had joined the table this evening, likely in place of his father, and was entertaining the group with stories of pirates and fierce storms he had sailed through in his youth. Jax listened with fascination, never having encountered a real live pirate before, but she knew the wilds of the Cetachi region were home to some of the most infamous and bloodthirsty hordes. Everyone seemed taken by the bold tales, with a flurry of questions peppering Jogan's descriptions.

Only Carriena seemed a bit subdued, hardly engaging in the evening. "Is everything all right?" Jax asked, with both concern for her friend and the possibility that she might uncover something useful to her pitiful investigation.

Carriena sighed, her cheek resting on a balled fist. "Jogan makes pirates seem so glamorous when they are nothing more than murderous brutes. They've been ransacking our seaside villages for the past few months," she sneered to no one in particular. "*Rose of the Sea* is not the only ship my father has had recently commissioned. We're in the process of building up our armada so that we can avenge our ravaged shores. So many of my people have lost everything because of those bastards. And he makes it sound like meeting them was fun!"

Jax was surprised by the surge of emotion Carriena displayed. For one who did not seem to care about ruling her duchy, she did obviously care deeply for her people. "I'm sure Jogan is just trying to keep everyone's mind off the fact that a dead man lies down the hall from their sleeping quarters."

Carriena's face whitened at the mention. "I suppose you're right. As you've likely guessed, I didn't tell anyone else how the banker really died," she said, her voice barely a whisper. "And considering how everyone has handled it thus far, I am inclined to believe Hazel has not broken her oath of secrecy." Carriena twirled her spoon between her slender fingers. "I will tell Valhalen once he's back on his feet tomorrow, and let him decide how to proceed."

Jax nodded in understanding. "Any news as to when the weather will turn around in our favor?" She dearly wanted the ship to resume sailing across the glassy waters.

"Jogan said earlier there were some growing clouds that looked like they might bring the wind with them, but it seems they have vanished from the night's sky," Carriena replied, rather glumly. "Perhaps for my birthday, I'll receive the breeze as a gift from the Virtues."

Jax smiled tightly, placing a hand over her friend's arm, a gesture she hoped appeared natural and not forced. "What a gift it would be."

As Carriena's narrowed eyes roamed over Jax's face, the Duchess did her best to keep her expression neutral. "I think I'm going to go back to my stateroom early. I've had enough of this day." Pushing her chair back, Carriena left the table without a word. Everyone's eyes fell to Jax, each probably wondering what she had said to make their hostess retreat so suddenly.

Ignoring their questioning stares, Jax cleared her throat. "Lady Giovanna, would it be too much to ask you to sing a few pieces from your father's show *On the High Seas*? I think it would be a lovely follow-up to Jogan's pirate tales."

The young actress's face beamed at the suggestion. "Oh, what a wonderful idea, Your Grace. I'm sorry I didn't think to offer it up first." She stood, motioning for everyone to follow her into the ballroom.

Perry pulled her into the corner of the emptying dining hall, concerned. "What happened between you and Carriena?"

Jax sighed, watching as Uma and Hendrie disappeared through the double doors, leaving them alone. "I'm not entirely sure. I think this journey is taking its toll on her. Whether it be guilt or nerves, I really don't know."

"Guilt? So, you really think she's behind all this misfortune?" Perry asked in obvious surprise.

"I thought about it all afternoon. As much as it tears my heart in two, I really don't see any other logical explanation."

He looked at her for a long moment, his eyes revealing a true sadness behind them. "I'm so sorry you're having to go through this, my love, but whatever the outcome of this voyage, just know that I will always be here by your side."

Although he had not said as much, she knew what sorrow he was referring to. The pain of losing a trusted friend was still so raw in her heart. If Carriena turned out to be behind all this, how was she going to cope with another betrayal? Was everyone in her inner circle destined to deceive her at some point? Was that the life she'd been resigned to as Duchess of Saphire?

Chapter Ten

Jax awoke the next morning, her spirits lifting from the previous night. Not only did she intend to determine the identity of the guilty party, but she could tell from the gentle rocking of the ship that they were skimming across the crystalline waters once more. With any luck, they would be pulling into port by tomorrow evening.

"Did you sleep well, dear one?" Jax asked with a chirp as Uma opened the door to her side chamber bedroom. Her lady's maid looked surprised that Jax was already up and wide awake.

"I did, and it appears you did as well. You're never this friendly in the morning," Uma teased, clearly relieved that the tension from the previous evening had all but evaporated.

"I'll ignore that slight. I am too giddy at the fact that we are once more moving toward Isla DeLacqua. I want to get off this ship." Trapped on board with a murderer was one thing, but the fact of the matter was that Jax hated feeling caged. She liked having the freedom to go out and about as she pleased, and since becoming Duchess, that freedom didn't seem so real anymore. Being confined to the borders of a boat only intensified her agitation.

"It's a shame we were delayed. I bet Lady Carriena was looking forward to celebrating her birthday on land," Uma said as she helped Jax into a lace-trimmed golden gown.

"I imagine Monsieur Devoyier will orchestrate a wonderful feast tonight in her honor. This way, she'll get to celebrate twice. I'm sure the Duke wouldn't pass up the chance to host a regal ball for his daughter, if it meant he could showcase his duchy for important guests," Jax said with a smirk.

To her delight, as she walked out of her suite, Jax ran into Captain Valhalen, who, although a bit pale, appeared nearly back to normal. "Duchess! It is a gift from the Virtues to see your beautiful face first thing in the morning. After being cared for by my son, it's a relief to see something other than his haggard features."

Jax grinned at the dashing older man. "I am thrilled to see you up and about, Captain. Have you made a full recovery?"

"Yes, almost. I feel foolish that I let myself be drugged by laced water. I was surprised at how long it took that blasted cloveroot to work its way out of my system, but I am happy to report I am more than able to command the ship."

"Jogan did a wonderful job in your stead, Captain," Jax praised.

At this comment, though, Valhalen's weathered face darkened. "Not good enough, if there has been stealing and murder going on under his watch."

Jax remembered that Carriena had planned to tell Valhalen the true cause of Grandeair's death. "I take it that Lady Carriena spoke to you already this morning?"

"It was hardly dawn when the poor woman came in. She's in a sorry state, if you don't mind me being so forward, Duchess. I know she's your friend from school; it might do her some good to have a bit of fun with everything happening around us." Valhalen's peppery gray eyebrows drew together, giving Jax a knowing look. "It's certainly not been the maiden voyage we expected, that's for sure."

Immediately, Jax's heart swelled for her friend. How awful the woman must feel after all that had happened during a cruise that was supposed to be a celebration. "I'll see if I can find her and help take her mind off things."

"Excellent. I'm going to have a word with my crew and see if I can rustle up any information that your Captain Solomon was not able to squeeze out of them," the sea captain said with a growl before making determined strides down the hallway.

Jax considered his words and moments later found herself knocking on Carriena's door. "This is your birthday wakeup call!"

After a few beats of silence, the young woman's ashen face appeared in the crack of the door. "I don't feel like celebrating, Jax."

"Nonsense." Jax pushed her way through, waltzing into the Rose Suite. "Remember what we used to do at school when either of us was feeling down?"

"Raid Professor Keelnori's mead cabinet?" Carriena said with a smirk, unable to resist Jax's prodding.

"No! We'd raid each other's closets and try everything on." Jax's eyes landed on the large boudoir near the regal canopy bed. "You must have a few extra items tucked away in that monstrous piece."

Carriena's eyes lit up with genuine excitement. "I did do quite a bit of shopping in Tandora's port city. Come on, I'll show you."

Quite a bit of shopping had resulted in Carriena purchasing eighteen new gowns. The two friends spent most of the morning, breakfast long forgotten, trying on the delicate fashions and modeling them for one another. Jax was pleased by the color returning to Carriena's cheeks, the birthday girl's eyes bright once more.

"That looks exquisite on you, dearest," Jax exclaimed, truly mesmerized by the elegant evening gown Carriena now showcased.

Twirling in the dazzling sunlight streaming in from the balcony windows, Carriena finished with a curtsy, gentling lift the blue satin sash from her waist. "Why thank you, I thought so as well. It's an original Voltistè."

Voltistè. Voltistè. Why did that name bounce around in Jax's mind so stubbornly? "I'm ashamed to say that I have not heard of that designer."

Carriena whirled around once more. "Actually, you have. You probably just didn't know they were one and the same. Voltistè is Florence Haulsinger's family name. She used it professionally after she married into the Haulsinger house."

"Florence Haulsinger is Voltistè?" Jax's mouth dropped open.

Carriena snorted a laugh. "I know, it's hard to believe, right? The fact that she can design such lovely creations but still be so frigid in person is beyond me."

But Jax was no longer listening. Florence Voltistè. *F. Voltistè.* The name she had seen in Monsieur Grandeair's ledger! Rushing out of Carriena's suite, Jax ran to Perry's door, pounding fiercely against the emerald-encrusted wood. A startled Hendrie greeted her, only to be barreled over as she ran straight to the mahogany desk where Perry said he'd secured the accounts ledger.

Thumbing through the pages with trembling anticipation, she found the missing piece to all the puzzles that had been laid out before her. For nearly twenty-five years, F. Voltistè had been paying back a twenty-thousand-gold loan to Monsieur Grandeair with interest so high, Jax wondered how it was legal. Each payment was meticulously recorded, every year, the payments growing larger and larger. Lady Florence must have paid Grandeair nearly three times the amount he loaned her back in the days when she must have been trying to start her tailoring business. From her shabby appearance, and frankly unremarkable jewelry collection, he must have been bleeding her dry.

Perry's casual words echoed in her head. Not a single name rings any bells. If it did, we'd have our killer. The amount that man forced people to pay him in return was murder itself.

Jax sat down, oblivious to both Hendrie's questions about whether she was feeling all right and Carriena's confused arrival into the room. The Duchess merely let the rest of the story unfold for her. She should have thought to question the guards more astutely after she had her run in with Lady Giovanna emerging from her brother's room. From down the long passage, in the dim light, it honestly looked to Jax as if the singer had emerged from Master Archer's cabin. But the illusion of light and depth tricked her, just as it must have tricked the guards the night Monsieur Grandeair was killed. She had been so caught up in figuring out how they could have missed someone going into the banker's room that she totally overlooked the fact that they did witness it. Only, they saw what they thought they *should* be seeing.

Lady Florence left dinner in an outrage that night, Sebastián and Eduardo reporting that she went right into her room. From their post at the end of the passageway, they could have easily made the same mistake Jax did. Lady Florence did not go into her own chambers; she would have picked the lock with a dress or hairpin, just as Jax had, and gone directly into Grandeair's room. Sebastián and Eduardo would have assumed from a distance that she was simply struggling to unlock her own door, which wouldn't have been hard to believe, given the condition her husband said her hands were in. Jax doubted Lady Florence was suffering from any type of acute hand pain, considering the beautiful creation Carriena modeled for her moments ago. It was all an act to fool everyone, even her decrepitly old and cruel husband.

As the evening wore on, Grandeair left the ballroom early, returning to his cabin where the guards saw him enter and shut the door. What likely happened was Florence closing the door herself, before lunging at Grandeair and stabbing him with all the fury she'd been harboring for twenty-five years. Even with her success as a renowned designer, the interest Grandeair was charging her for an under-the-table loan was more than enough to cripple her from truly advancing into financial prosperity. Knowing that the man before her was responsible for her hopeless lot in life, Jax did not have to wonder how the old woman was able to summon the strength to plunge the dinner knife she had stolen from the luncheon repeatedly into the moneylender's flesh.

Once he was dead at her feet, Lady Florence simply waited until she heard everyone else come back from the ballroom. At that point, she emerged from the last door on the left, the narrow walls tricking everyone into thinking she was actually coming out of the second to last door, her own. There, she apologized and made peace with the guests, no one suspecting that her dark red gown was masking a trail of blood, an ensemble chosen thoughtfully before dinner for that very reason. She then finally entered her own room for the first time that night, her plan executed to near perfection. If only she had thought to find and dispose of the ledger, it would have been impossible to prove her guilt.

Lady Florence Haulsinger had tricked them all. Jax was ashamed to note that the elderly noblewoman never had been seriously considered a suspect, one because of her apparent age and, two, because she had been a victim herself.

The brooch. The telltale crime that started it all. It had been a ruse right from the very start. By orchestrating the missing brooch, Lady Florence masterfully linked the two crimes together. Who would steal an old woman's heirloom and then kill a banker? The fact that no one was seen by the guards entering Lady Florence's room was another factor in causing Jax to pursue the wild theory that someone was climbing the sides of the ship to commit these acts, when in fact, there had never been any crime at all. No one was seen entering cabin seven to take the brooch because no one actually did. Jax wondered what had really happened to the piece. Had Lady Florence simply thrown it out the window into the open arms of the sea? She supposed only one person knew the truth to that question.

As for the cloveroot and its role in poisoning Captain Valhalen, Jax remembered the offhanded comments of Ernest Haulsinger, something she barely paid attention to due to her own fears of her lies being revealed. After Vincent told Jax where Perry could replenish his supply of cloveroot in Beautraud, Ernest had rudely grumbled that they had traveled through the duchy on their way to Tafreeni's port. Lady Florence must have acquired the poison at that point. She had arrived early to the ship and likely was able to slip the root into the Captain's water before the guards started paying close attention to their posts.

It all fell into place in Jax's mind so effortlessly that she couldn't believe she hadn't figured it out sooner.

"Jax! Are you having a seizure of some sort?" Perry's panicked voice finally claimed her attention.

She blinked a few times, taking in the worried expressions around her. Carriena and Hendrie had been joined by an anxious Perry, George, Uma, and Jogan. Hazel and Charles both appeared in the doorway of the Emerald Suite, Hazel with her bag of herbs and Charles with a thick medical tome. "I'm fine. I'm fine!" she protested, holding her hands up in reassurance. "I'm so sorry to have frightened you, but I just got lost in my thoughts."

"What in the name of the Virtues were you thinking about?" Carriena shrieked, tears of relief flowing freely from her eyes. "We thought you'd gone into a trance or something dreadful."

"I guess it was a bit of a trance," Jax chuckled, making light of the situation. "My mind was piecing everything together so quickly that the rest of me hardly had time to catch up."

Perry's eyebrows raised. "Piecing everything together? Jax, have you figured out what's been happening on this cursed ship?"

Jax smiled suggestively, beaming already with pride. "Oh, I think I have."

Chapter Eleven

Without another word of explanation, Jax motioned the assembled passengers to follow her to the main deck. Ernest Haulsinger and his wife were sitting up near the bow of the ship, each engrossed in a book.

"Greetings to you both," Jax said brightly while the others behind her exchanged questioning glances.

Ernest grumbled a reply, not even bothering to look up from his text. Lady Haulsinger, however, looked up at the Duchess and smiled warmly in return. "Hello, Duquessa. Are you enjoying the weather today? It's wonderful the breeze has returned."

"Yes, I am enjoying it. Gives me some time to sink my teeth into a riveting read." Jax held up a small leather-bound book in her hands.

The way Lady Haulsinger's smile lost its luster told Jax the woman recognized the ledger. "I found this little book in Monsieur Grandeair's quarters. It paints quite the interesting story. Care to share your version of events, Florence Voltistè?"

She felt Perry stiffen beside her as he put the pieces together before her other companions, no doubt recognizing the name from his review of the notes.

The rosy red flush drained from the elegant woman's face, leaving a pale, haunting look. "You have no proof." Her words were ice.

Jax challenged her triumphantly. "I think if we search your cabin, we will find the beautiful red gown you wore the night you murdered Monsieur Grandeair, a gown you designed specifically to mask the victim's blood. Perhaps, if you decided to keep it as a souvenir, we'll also find the dinner knife you stole to plunge into his back. And let's not forget the cloveroot to poison our dear captain. Or did you throw everything overboard like you did your beloved brooch?"

Lady Florence pursed her lips as she grimly looked at the assembled faces before her. Vincent, Giovanna, and Archer had joined them all up on the bow, curious as to what was unraveling.

"Admit it," Jax ordered. "Grandeair had been hustling you for nearly three decades, and you saw this voyage as an opportunity to seek vengeance. Grandeair only knew you as *F. Voltistè*. He had no idea what you looked like, as he never conducted business with his clients face-to-face, or that your married name was Haulsinger. He likely let it slip in his financial correspondence that he was invited on the inaugural journey of *Rose of the Sea*, and when you received an invitation as well, you must have thought the Virtues were smiling down upon you."

Lady Florence continued to stare without feeling at the open waters.

Jax pushed onward, hoping to jar the truth out of the woman. "You traveled through Beautraud and secured cloveroot, the first step in your plan to render the Captain ill, so that he could not use his authority to interfere with your plans. You didn't expect anyone else on board to care enough to investigate the unfortunate events that were about to unfold, so once you laced the Captain's water, you waited a day for it to take effect before feigning your brooch being stolen." With a triumphant smile, she continued. "You didn't expect me and my companions to take your claims seriously and begin investigating. But I must say, Florence Voltistè, you fooled us well. We were so blinded by this phantom who stole your brooch that we hardly got in your way. You were still able to execute Monsieur Grandeair, and you were even seen by the guards leaving his room! But the unfortunate illusion caused by the design of the narrow corridor gave you the perfect alibi, as they thought you were coming out of your own room. Everything was going according to plan. Except you left this behind… a record of the money you've paid to Grandeair all these years." The Duchess held up the incriminating ledger. "I would never have put the pieces together otherwise."

"Well, it is wonderful to know that my greatest masterpiece was still a complete failure," the old woman spat bitterly, causing Jax to wonder how long she had been planning her revenge.

Lady Florence's cold stare met her own. "Congratulations on another mystery solved, Duquessa. I hope you are satisfied." With lightning speed, Lady Florence took them all off guard as she dashed madly to the railing, throwing her body into the dark arms of the sea.

"No!" Jax screamed, lunging forward a moment too late, Florence Voltistè's dress slipping from her outstretched fingers. She felt herself tip forward, her balance thwarted by the rough waves.

Perry's strong arm encircled her waist with ferocity, pulling her back from the railing. "Careful, Jax. She's gone. Don't let her madness take you with her."

Trembling with a rush of emotions, Jax buried her head into Perry's shoulder, trying to erase the wild look she saw on Florence Voltistè's face as the waters dragged her beneath the surface into a cold and wet grave.

Chapter Twelve

It had not been a pleasant task to wake Ernest Haulsinger up from his impromptu nap, as the old man had fallen asleep right next to his wife while the whole ordeal unfolded. While not particularly fond of the uncouth elder, Jax felt her chest tighten as she watched genuine despair fill his wrinkly face when he was told of his wife's untimely death. He excused himself from the main deck, asking the Captain if he might be able to take his meals in his room for the remainder of the journey. Carriena answered for the Captain, telling him that he could.

It took the passengers of *Rose of the Sea* hours to calm down after witnessing the takedown of Monsieur Grandeair's killer. Jax answered a myriad of questions from the guests, each in awe of what she had uncovered over the course of her investigation. Since most had been oblivious to the cause of death being murder, Jax fielded many questions about who had been suspected of the devious crime.

"At one time, you were quite high on the list," Jax joked with an astonished Charles as his sister clung to his arm. Lady Giovanna had followed him around like a shadow since the events on the main deck, something Jax noted Charles was quite happy about.

‡

"While I know I should be mad at you for suspecting me, I know what Arnie's betrayal did to you, Jax, and for that, I'm truly sorry," Carriena said later that evening, when the two women sat on the top deck under the starry sky. She reached over and squeezed Jax's hand affectionately.

"I knew deep down you were innocent, dear one. I'm just so sorry I let my insecurities get the better of my judgment," Jax revealed, apologizing in her own right.

"I never should have been worried that this all wouldn't work out," Carriena said, her eyes shimmering under the moon's rays. "I thought all these terrible things would destroy Isla DeLacqua's chances at forging stronger relations. But to my surprise, Ernest Haulsinger has agreed to convince Duke Savant to lower the clothing tax in exchange for a formal declaration that he was in no way, shape, or form involved with his wife's dastardly deeds. Lady Giovanna and Sir Charles are going to use their influence to help negotiate a better wine price, something that Lady Giovanna will personally oversee herself. I guess this means she'll be visiting Isla DeLacqua quite a bit in the future, something I think she and her brother are both happy about."

"That's wonderful to hear, Carriena. And I know Hazel and Vincent have offered their help, and plan to speak with the leaders of the Ancient Faith throughout your duchy. You should be proud of everything you have accomplished," Jax praised her friend, truly impressed by the success Isla DeLacqua had come by after this horrid ordeal.

"I owe it all to you, my true *Rose of the Sea*," Carriena bowed her head and her arms forward in playful worship, chanting Jax's name repeatedly. "None of this would have happened without your interference."

"Interference? Is that really what you're calling it?" the Duchess exclaimed, laughing with indignation.

"Well, no, I suppose *I'm* the one who actually interfered." Carriena suddenly sprang to her feet, looking toward the staircase to the main deck. "I'll leave you two alone." She winked and skipped down the wooden platform, moving past to reveal Perry standing there, looking incredibly nervous.

"What's this about?" Jax demanded, taken off guard by his presence.

"I've been so stupid, Jax." Perry rushed forward, taking her hands in his, pulling her to her feet. She felt his heart beating wildly underneath his strong chest. "Thank the Virtues Carriena set me straight. I thought you were the one who needed to do this. I feel like a complete idiot."

"Do what? Perry, what are you talking about?" Jax felt the cold grip of panic on her heart. Had the sea taken his mind, too?

Before her, Perry dropped to one knee, the moonlight dancing on his dark hair, the breeze ruffling his curls. "Duchess Jacqueline Arienta Xavier, from the moment I saw you, I knew you were the fiercest, most beautiful creature I'd ever seen. When I found out our fathers arranged our marriage, I was genuinely frightened, for how could such a breathtaking force of nature ever come to care for someone unremarkable like me? I was disappointed because I wanted to marry for love. I was scared because you are a powerful Duchess and I am a seventh son with no real title to my name. But the Virtues blessed me, for reasons I still question to this day. I found myself enjoying your company unlike anyone ever before. I found my own confidence in your faith in me. I found myself falling in love with you, and you nearly burst my heart when you told me you loved me too."

Too stunned to speak, Jax stood, her mouth agape, watching Perry's eyes fill with tears. "I am so sorry it's taken me this long to ask. I honestly was waiting for you to do it, since I know how much you like to be in charge. But goodness, Jax, will you please make me the happiest man in the realm and be my wife?"

There was nothing Jax could or wanted to say, other than "Yes."

Chapter Thirteen

The hard, sturdy ground felt like sable carpet beneath Jax's feet. It had taken a few moments for her to adjust to the absence of movement beneath her, but she found her pace quickly as Lord Pettraud, her fiancé, escorted her off the causeway of *Rose of the Sea*. Her luxurious home for the past five days nestled in its slip within Isla DeLacqua's harbor, looking as majestic as the day she had first laid eyes on it.

The wind had been good to them for the remainder of the voyage, the sun just only beginning to set in the western sky as they pulled into port. While everyone on board was in high spirits after the intense experience they'd all survived together, Jax could see by the way they all crowded around the causeway that they were eager to be on dry, steady land.

Walking ahead of them on Captain Solomon's arm, Lady Carriena turned back to give the engaged couple a bursting look of happiness. "I am so excited for you both!" she squealed for the hundredth time since they'd entered the harbor.

"I never would have guessed," Perry said with a straight face before they all dissolved into laughter.

The lightness in Jax's heart was foreign to her. It had been a long time since she'd had any real reason to truly celebrate, and now, with her beloved on her arm and her friends all around her, she wished this moment could last forever.

"It's going to be quite a wild tale to tell my father, for sure." Carriena sighed, a little warily, waving to the distant figure of Duke DeLacqua, waiting for her and her party up near the harbor's landing. "If I knew you'd cause such trouble aboard, I never would have invited you," she teased, tossing a playful look at Jax.

Looking first at Uma, Hendrie, George, and Perry, Jax couldn't help but blush. "I guess we do tend to get ourselves into trouble."

Pulling her close under his arm, Perry kissed the top of her forehead. "And we'll always pull ourselves out of it. Together."

Jax gave him a secret smile. "Together."

~BONUS CONTENT~

This edition includes the Realm of Virtues story, **Ruined Remnants**. *In this delightful tale, readers are invited to join Jax and Perry on their engagement tour, which takes place after their harrowing seabound journey in* **A Voyage of Vengeance**.

Far from the intense mysteries and perilous encounters they've faced, this lighthearted adventure offers a refreshing change of pace. As Jax and Perry traverse picturesque landscapes and historic ruins, their bond grows stronger, and they find joy in shared moments of discovery and laughter.

Yet, this tale is more than just a romantic getaway; it lays important groundwork for the series, hinting at the challenges that lie ahead for the couple.

Ruined Remnants

~A Realm of Virtues Story~

Sarah E. Burr

Chapter One

Duchess Jacqueline Arienta Xavier rested her head on her fiancé's shoulder, enjoying the feel of his strong, solid form almost as much as the simple pleasure of calling Lord Percival Pettraud her betrothed.

"What a perfect day," she murmured as warm rays tickled her sun-kissed cheeks through the carriage window.

"A perfect day, week, month." Perry chuckled, the sound rumbling from deep within his chest. He lifted her hand to his lips. "This really has been the most glorious summer."

Jax straightened and assessed her fiancé's appearance. The Saphire sun had altered his normally pale skin to a buttery gold, but his wild mess of dark curls remained ever the same, if a little longer. She reached for a tendril, twirling it around her finger. "I don't want it to end."

"Neither do I, but I suppose we can't live inside a carriage forever." Perry motioned to their luxurious surroundings. "Even one so grand as this."

The weight of his words rested heavily on her. No, they could not. She had a nation to oversee, matters of state to address. The Duchy of Saphire needed its Duchess to return home, and soon. High Courtier Jaquobie had granted Jax this brief respite, attending to the duchy's day-to-day administration whilst Jax toured her beloved homeland with her new fiancé. But Jaquobie had sent urgent word this morning. There were rumblings in the north from the wilds of Cetachi, a lawless region in the Realm of Virtues with no rule or ruler. That might all change, for Jaquobie's spies had learned of a lone man who had ignited a political movement that now spread rapidly throughout Cetachi. It was a movement that threatened to upend the very ideals with which the Realm of Virtues was governed. No, she and her darling Perry could not remain on tour forever. The realm's issues called her back.

"Then we must make the most of this final leg of the journey." Jax threaded her fingers through Perry's and stroked them with gentle anticipation.

Her fiancé glanced out the carriage window, surveying the lush woodlands that surrounded them. "A bit off the beaten path, aren't we?"

Jax giggled. "Rothgart is one of the southern-most cities in Saphire. It takes a while to get there. But fear not; their legendary chocolate swill will be worth it."

"Ha! How can anything called 'swill' be worth it?" Perry shook his head with a snort.

Just the memory of the rich chocolate drink made Jax's tastebuds tingle with desire. "Never judge a drink by its name, my love."

They settled into companionable silence as the carriage continued its sojourn. Throughout the summer, she and Perry had traveled across the duchy, introducing the people of Saphire to their future Prince Consort. The trip had also served an educational purpose, allowing Perry to learn all he could about the dukedom he would one day help Jax support. Their last stop on this grand tour across the nation was the border city of Rothgart.

Jax gazed out her window, taking in the beautiful view of her duchy. It never failed to leave her breathless. Arching, tall trees shaded them with a lush green canopy. Through the breaks in the forest wall, she spied a grassy meadow carpeted with wildflowers. A pond shimmered in the distance, sunlight refracting off the crystal blue surface.

A little while later, just as sleep tugged at her eyelids, her amethyst gaze caught sight of a crooked signpost sprouting off a beaten pathway. "Wait a moment. Stop!" Jax pounded her fist on the coach door.

Perry jumped in his seat, spooked awake by her cry. "Are you all right?" He hurriedly wiped sleep from his eyes.

Before Jax could answer, a shadow appeared in her side window as the carriage rolled to a halt. "What is it, Jax?" Captain George Solomon's warm chocolate eyes narrowed with concern as he assessed her and Perry.

"That signpost back there." Jax pointed a finger out the window. "It mentions the Hamlet of Favored Crossing. That settlement is not mentioned on our itinerary."

The afternoon sun danced across George's tan skin. "No, it is not." He spoke as if stating the obvious.

Jax wrinkled her brow at him. "Well, why not? I thought this tour was meant to include all settlements within Saphire."

George shrugged. "I was not the one who put together this tour, Duchess," he reminded her. "Your courtiers did."

Jax's frown grew more severe at the oversight. Favored Crossing might be a small hamlet, but its people were still her citizens. They deserved the same attention as every other village, town, and city within the duchy. "Well, I'd like to believe that Favored Crossing was unintentionally overlooked when mapping out our travels. We must change course at once."

Now it was the Captain of the Ducal Guard's turn to frown. "Rothgart is expecting our arrival this evening."

"Then please send a messenger ahead, and let them know we'll be delayed a few hours," Jax instructed, not one to be easily swayed.

George reached for the back of his neck, annoyance dancing across his handsome features. "We only have a few hours of daylight left, and I will not risk the ducal caravan traveling the roads after sundown."

"Fine. Then we shall stay the night in Favored Crossing. The celebration doesn't commence until tomorrow afternoon, anyway." Rothgart was set to host a grand festival in honor of Jax and Perry's engagement.

Perry cleared his throat, glancing sheepishly at Jax. "Dearest, I'm not sure a place as small as a hamlet would have accommodations suitable for a Duchess."

George grunted agreement.

Jax rolled her eyes at their lack of enthusiasm. "We haven't spent the last two and half months traveling the *entire* duchy only to skip over *one* settlement. Come now, where's your sense of adventure? We have tents packed, after all, if there's no place for us to sleep."

George rubbed at his temples. Jax was evidently giving him a headache with her demands. "If it's that important to you —"

"It is," Jax confirmed. "I cannot have any of my people feeling as though they don't matter to their Duchess." She glanced down the worn side path leading toward Favored Crossing. The name did not ring an immediate bell, and she was ashamed that she had not realized one of her holdings had been left off their trip's itinerary. If Jax had fallen asleep in the carriage, like Perry, she would have been none the wiser.

George stared at her a moment, clearly debating with himself on how to proceed. "As you wish, Duchess. I'll send riders to alert Rothgart that we'll arrive tomorrow before noon."

Jax reached out the open window to grasp George's forearm. "Thank you."

He simply blew a gust of air over his lips in response. "Lieutenant!" he called to one of the hundred soldiers surrounding the ducal caravan. "Send a trio of your men to Rothgart and alert them of a delay. I also need a squad to ride ahead and scout the hamlet southeast of here, as well—Favored Crossing. Inform the settlement that their Duchess will be making an impromptu visit."

As the Ducal Guard rallied around their captain outside the confines of the carriage, Jax sank back into her seat, a triumphant smile painted across her face.

Perry shook his head, his curls swinging as he chuckled. "So much for chocolate swill."

Chapter Two

The carriage lurched forward once more. Jax narrowly avoided smashing into Perry as she careened sideways in her seat.

Perry wrapped a steadying arm around her shoulder. "Bumpy ride, eh?" He gave her a charming, crooked grin.

Before she could respond, the carriage shuddered violently again before coming to a halting stop. George appeared in the window not a heartbeat later.

"This path is too rough for the caravan to continue." He motioned down the road they had been traveling. "The carriages will need new axels if we go any further."

"How far are we from Favored Crossing?" Jax leaned out the window to survey the surrounding forest that loomed around them.

"The scouts say about fifteen minutes by foot. Are you up for a walk?" George cocked his head in an amused challenge. "I'd like to let the horses rest in that glade over there."

Jax didn't bother looking in the direction he indicated. She was already gathering her skirts. "Of course. We've worked the poor creatures hard enough as is." She tossed a look over her shoulder at Perry. "You don't mind taking a brisk stroll, do you, darling?"

Perry gathered the small travel satchel at his feet. "The fresh air will do me good."

Jax turned to George. "All we need is a few moments to gather our belongings for an overnight stay."

"That won't be necessary, Jax. We've already packed everything." Uma Dorrow stepped into view from behind George, holding two ornate saddlebags in her hands. Beside her, Hendrie Dumont mirrored her, clutching bags of his own.

Jax smiled gratefully at her lady's maid. "I should have known you'd be prepared." She dipped her chin in thanks to Hendrie, Perry's longtime valet, as well.

Uma tucked a strand of mousy brunette hair behind her ear. "Are you sure this overnight visit is wise? George told us you were prepared to sleep in tents if it came to it," she said with a shudder.

Jax climbed out of the carriage unassisted, eager to get a move on. "Well, dear one, *that's* only because George refuses to allow the caravan to travel at night." She paused, her amethyst gaze trailing to the three transports behind her own that made up their royal procession. Uma and Hendrie had traveled in the first, while the other two served as luggage transports for their entire envoy. "And *I* refuse to miss out on visiting Favored Crossing. Spending the night is the only way to accommodate both our needs."

Uma's lips pressed together. "Your stubbornness is going to be the death of me."

"You took the words right out of my mouth, Uma." George shook his head with a sigh. "I'm leaving behind a segment of the Ducal Guard to mind the carriages and horses. They'll make camp in the glade. The rest will accompany us to Favored Crossing."

Jax took one of the bags Uma carried. "Lead on, Captain." She was glad she had worn her favorite laced boots under her elegant gold gown. She could walk in comfort while still presenting herself to the people of Favored Crossing as their regal Duchess.

A formation of thirty soldiers swarmed around Jax and her companions, serving as a protective barrier. Though, the forest was so still and silent, Jax wasn't sure there was anything out there she needed protection from.

Perry took her hand in his, and their modified royal procession resumed their trek down the dusty path, stepping to avoid deep ruts every few feet or so.

"This road is in horrible condition," Jax muttered to herself.

Concern began to unfurl in her chest. Why hadn't the people of Favored Crossing sent a request to the regional courtier to address this? Matters such as these should be brought forward and attended to by the advisors in her court.

Up ahead, one of her soldiers stumbled and issued a low curse likely not meant for his Duchess's ears.

"Captain," another member of the Guard asked, "are you sure we took the right turn off?"

George, who had hiked a few paces ahead of Jax and Perry, turned his head to the side so that Jax could see the deep frown etched into his tan face. "This is the only path marked on the map. It's likely neglected from infrequent use. I doubt this hamlet sees many travelers. It's quite remote."

Silence descended over their group as they continued, the trees growing thicker all around them.

"Do you hear that?" Perry whispered after a few minutes, his lavender eyes narrowed in concentration.

Jax listened intently. "No. What do you hear?"

"That's just it." Perry surveyed the woods around them. "Nothing. No birds, no animals. No sounds of activity from the village."

Shadows stretched across their path. The late afternoon sun was barely able to penetrate the thick canopy of leaves overhead. "You're right," Jax murmured. "It's *too* quiet."

"It's spooky, is what it is." Behind them, Uma leaned into Hendrie, clutching his free arm. "I've never even heard of Favored Crossing. Are you sure it's a real place?"

Jax giggled, hoping to ease the nerves evident in Uma's pinched expression. "Of course, it is, dear one." She opened her mouth to share something about the hamlet, some fact about its land or people, but she realized she couldn't summon a word. How could she not know anything about one of her own holdings? Jax took great pride in her extensive knowledge of her duchy and its people, so why had her mind gone blank when she thought of Favored Crossing? She shook her head. Perhaps it was just due to fatigue from the trip.

Several moments of uneasy silence passed before Jax noted the smell of smoke in the air. Her gaze traveled upward to a break in the forest canopy, and she spied swirling gray tendrils rising into the sky ahead of their party. Soon, thatched rooftops appeared, and as the forest began to thin out around them, a settlement emerged up ahead. Jax counted fifteen structures in her line of sight, much more than she had originally expected.

A stone wall ran around the outer edge of the hamlet, with a large brick archway serving as an entrance. A sea of faces greeted the party at the arch, and Jax guessed Favored Crossing's entire population had assembled to welcome them.

"Oh, my. It *is* true!" a girlish voice called from the crowd. "Those scouts weren't pulling our leg."

"It really is her," a chorus of replies rippled through the bubbling excitement.

"Virtues praise our glorious Duchess!"

A hearty cheer followed, and in a smooth motion, the people of Favored Crossing dropped into a reverent kneel.

The Ducal Guard parted so that Jax could glide forward and acknowledge her citizens, but before she could greet them, an old man in worn but well-made robes rushed forward.

George swooped in and stepped in front of Jax before the old man could reach her, placing a firm hand on the stranger's shoulder.

The elder did not seem to even realize George had intervened. His brown eyes stared fervently at Jax. "Duchess! Have you come to save us?"

Chapter Three

Jax went rigid, stunned by the man's question. "Save you? From what?"

The color drained from his wrinkled face. "From the phantom." His words were a gritty hiss.

Jax shared an apprehensive look with Perry. What in the Virtues was this man talking about?"

"Step back from your Duchess, sir," George said, his left hand guiding the man backward. Jax noted George's right hand rested on the hilt of his sword, ready to spring into action.

"Forgive me. I—I am sorry for my outburst." The old man's eyes watered. "Your arrival here is the first real hope we've had in weeks."

Jax's gaze darted to the rest of the gathered crowd. What she had assumed was excitement about her visit was a gross misinterpretation. Relief and hope mingled on the expressions that greeted her, but another feeling dominated each face—fear. "Please explain what you mean." She turned her attention to the old man. "Sir…?"

"I am Yuryk Huffingson, Your Grace. I serve as the Speaker of Favored Crossing."

Jax nodded in understanding. A Speaker acted as an unofficial liaison between a village and its assigned courtier. Often, a village elder took on the role. "Greetings, Speaker Yuryk. It is a pleasure to meet you. I am Duchess Jacqueline." She felt the need to introduce herself in a less formal capacity.

Yuryk dropped into a low bow. "The honor is all mine, Your Grace. But, unfortunately, we have unhappy tidings to discuss. Shall we continue this conversation inside? When we heard about your impending arrival, I arranged for food and wine in the brew house."

Hesitant, Jax glanced at George. The captain's expression was set in a grim stare. Unhappy tidings? Just what had they stumbled into here? "You're very kind, Speaker Yuryk," she said, acknowledging the invitation, "but we've brought our own refreshments." Jax motioned to two of the Ducal Guard who carried large packs on their back. Her envoy simply could not risk eating food without taking proper security measures—not after her beloved parents had been savagely poisoned. "Please, why don't you share the meal you've prepared with the people of Favored Crossing?"

"How gracious of you, Duchess." Yuryk again bent into a sweeping bow before turning to the assembled crowd. "Her Royal Highness requests that Favored Crossing enjoys a feast on her behalf."

Feeble applause met his announcement. The crowd was still very much on edge.

Yuryk continued, "Rest assured, my good people, the Ducal Guard will be able to protect us, now that they are here."

Jax swallowed back the unease lodged in her throat at such a weighty promise.

George did not react until the crowd began to disperse. Grabbing the Speaker by the elbow, he pulled the man close. "Protect you from what?" George, too, was clearly on edge about such a promise. The Ducal Guard was here to defend *her*, not an entire village.

Yuryk frowned, multiplying the wrinkles on his leathery face. "Haven't you come to save us from the phantom that torments our people?"

There was the man's use of the term phantom again. Jax wrinkled her brow in confusion. Her rational mind knew ghosts to be myths, used to scare children and the gullible alike. Ghosts weren't real, and certainly couldn't torment an entire hamlet. Still, her vivid imagination yearned to believe that the spirits of the dead roamed this realm. It made her feel closer to her dearly departed parents.

"Speaker Yuryk, we came to Favored Crossing to share our joyous news with you all." Jax took Perry by the hand and pulled him forward. "I am to wed Lord Percival of Pettraud, and Saphire is to have a new Prince Consort. Yet, it sounds as though you have more pressing matters that require our attention."

Yuryk's features tightened. "Yes, Your Grace. While I am honored you have traveled so far to share such happy news, I'm afraid the safety of Favored Crossing weighs heavily on the minds of all who live here."

Jax could practically see the wheels of anxiety spinning in George's head. No doubt, he wished to help Favored Crossing, but his duty was to keep Jax out of harm's reach. Well, she could make the choice somewhat easier for him. To Yuryk, Jax quickly replied, "Please, tell us how we can help."

From over the top of the Speaker's salt-and-pepper hair, George glared at her. He likely wanted to whisk her away from this place immediately. George wouldn't abandon these people in need, but he'd certainly rather Jax be removed from the situation before exploring their troubles. Which was precisely why she had inserted herself into the equation. She wasn't about to turn around and flee the moment her citizens asked for her aid.

Yuryk, unaware of the turmoil boiling between Jax and George's stubborn personalities, wrung his hands. "The mournful wails began a little over a month ago. They carried in the air from the ruins west of here, remnants of an old Ancient Faith temple from back before the Rebirth."

Jax's mouth dropped open in shock. She had no idea there were ancient remains of the Faith still located in Saphire. She thought they had all been torn down after the Faith's defeat some five hundred years ago. It was what she had been taught by her tutors and her father, Duke Richard.

"At first we thought it might be some wounded animal. I sent some scouts to survey the ruins, but once they arrived, the cries ceased." Yuryk's watery eyes widened. "They searched the portion of the ruins the wails had come from and found nothing. And yet, every night afterward, the moans have haunted the air. Soon, things around the hamlet began to go missing, vanishing without a trace. Food, at first, but then clothing began disappearing from laundry lines. Farming tools, too. The blacksmith's shop was also raided. But there has never been any trace of bandits. No footprints, no disturbances in the dirt or grass." Yuryk shook his head in slight disbelief. "All the while, the eerie cries and shrieks from the ruins have continued. I sent my most skilled hunters, hoping to recover our belongings. They found nothing about the fallen stone, although part of the temple crumbled, nearly crushing them. The ruins are dangerous to navigate, yet we know something lives there. We hear it in the wind."

"Some*thing* lives there?" Jax raised an eyebrow.

Yuryk nodded vigorously. "A phantom, Your Grace. An Ancient Faith spirit, trapped within that ruined temple."

"A phantom would not need food and tools, Speaker Yuryk." George looked like he was struggling to keep his stoic composure.

Jax had to agree with her captain.

Yuryk's eyes narrowed. "Then how do you explain the scene of each crime? There was no trace a human had been present."

"Perhaps you missed something."

Jax discreetly nudged George in the side. Nothing good would come from antagonizing the old man. "Speaker, when was the most recent incident?"

"Just this morning, Your Grace, at the blacksmith's forge. He refuses to go inside, so the scene remains untouched. You may examine the place, if you'd like. It's been left as the craftsman found it this morning." Yuryk lowered his voice, even though they were only surrounded by Jax's closest companions and guards. "We've heard tales of your exploits, Duchess, of the puzzles you solve. That's why I wrote to Courtier Gavant that we needed your assistance." His face drew into a frown. "But I never heard back."

While she wasn't pleased to hear this, Jax could imagine the circumstances as to why. If Courtier Gavant had received a missive from a small village, requesting the nation's Duchess drop everything to come help them rid themselves of a ghost…well, the tenured advisor would have gotten a good chuckle. If Yuryk hadn't let his imagination run away with him, Gavant would very well have instructed a squad of Saphire's armed forces to rid the hamlet of bandits.

But since the Virtues had delivered her here, Jax decided she could at least humor the poor man. She and the Ducal Guard would examine the forge, find evidence of bandits, then send a squad to deal with them.

Before she answered, George pulled her and Perry to the side. "If there are bandits roaming these woods, we need to get you both out of here." He kept his voice hushed so Yuryk could not overhear him.

Jax matched his tone. "Nonsense. I'm well enough protected, George. From the sounds of it, this *phantom* is only stealing enough food to feed one or two people. I'm sure the Ducal Guard can ward off a local bandit or two." She held his fiery gaze. "It would be prudent to resolve this issue for Favored Crossing, and quickly. I can't have word spreading that Saphire's Duchess turned away her people in their hour of need, *especially* after they made a plea to their Courtier." She would have words with Courtier Gavant when they eventually returned to the palace. His dismissal of this matter had put her in a difficult position, indeed.

George rubbed his temples. "So, my men do all the work, and *you* get the credit as the savior of Favored Crossing?" The corners of his lips twitched.

"I mean, if you'd rather I go traipsing about an ancient ruin—"

Her captain held up his hand. "Fine. I'll take some men to investigate the forge and see if we can pick up a trail."

"I might as well come with you, since Favored Crossing asked for *my* skills and all." Jax suppressed a victorious grin as she turned to the awaiting Yuryk. She did love a good puzzle, after all. "Very well, Speaker. I shall examine the forge. Lead the way."

Chapter Four

Curious faces stared at Jax from dust-covered windows as the Saphire envoy strode through the center of the hamlet. She realized she must look absurd to these people, surrounded by a horde of guardsmen in her fine gown, traipsing through such a rustic setting.

"Speaker Yuryk," Jax spoke up, claiming the man's attention as he led them down the row of sturdy structures, "my delegation will need to make camp for the night. Where would be convenient?"

Yuryk debated only a moment. "There's a clearing just north of here, Your Grace. Plenty of space for your men. Though, I insist you and Lord Pettraud take lodging in my family's home. It is humble, but it's dry and warm."

"I appreciate your generous offer, Speaker, but I cannot displace your family from their beds." Jax smiled at the man's kindness. "I will make camp with my soldiers. In fact…Uma? Hendrie? Why don't you go with some of the men and settle in? There's no need for thirty soldiers to examine the blacksmith's forge." She glanced at George to give his men the official order.

He sighed, although he did not refute her suggestion. "The Duchess makes a good point. Svenson, take your column and assist Uma and Hendrie with readying the campsite. Then get yourself some rest. Your men will take the night watch."

Svenson, a tall, muscled fighter, saluted his captain. "You heard 'im, boys." With that, he led fifteen men in the direction Yuryk had indicated.

Uma bit her lip, turning to Jax before she followed Svenson. "Be careful, Jax."

"We've never come up against a ghost before." Hendrie's throat wobbled.

Jax chuckled, remembering how she'd once thought a phantom could be their culprit when she and her friends had investigated a crime at sea. Of course, their offender had turned out to be very human.

Once Uma, Hendrie, and the assigned soldiers departed, Yuryk resumed leading their group toward a stout, one-story building. A massive chimney protruded from the rooftop, but no smoke bellowed from it today. The forge was quiet.

"I shall let you do your work," the Speaker said as he gestured to the front door of the shop, hanging slightly ajar.

Perry snorted and whispered to Jax, "A ghost wouldn't need to break down a door."

"Indeed." Jax's practiced gaze carefully assessed the front of the building. Besides the large door hanging crookedly on its hinges, the exterior of the forge was immaculately maintained.

George stepped forward and examined the door, swinging it back and forth with a critical stare. "Your phantom doesn't float through walls?" He gave a pointed look at the Speaker, clearly willing the man to see reason.

Yuryk swallowed. "Actually, Captain, the damage was caused by Craftmaster Hildaldo. Once he realized his forge had fallen victim to our phantom, the man panicked and crashed through the doorway."

At this news, Jax and Perry shared a frown. "How did the thief enter, then?" Jax pressed.

Yuryk shrugged. "There was no sign of forced entry, which was why Hildaldo was so shocked to find his forge in a state of disarray upon entering." He clasped his hands in front of him. "I'm afraid I have some other matters to attend to, Duchess, but please feel free to come find me in my home. It's the one with a painted blue door."

Jax smiled in farewell, turning to George once the Speaker was out of earshot. "Perhaps the bandit came through one of the windows?" There were three large windows facing frontward, and Jax was sure there would be more, to keep the forge properly ventilated.

George muttered words to seven of his men, and they took off around the building. "These three don't appear to be disturbed." George stroked the dark stubble on his chin before opening the broken door and disappearing inside the forge.

Jax and Perry followed him, leaving behind the eight remaining guards to investigate the exterior.

Perry stopped short upon entering. "A rather tidy workspace for a blacksmith. Doesn't look like he's even been robbed."

Jax assessed the scene herself, her gaze running along the many tables of weapons and tools. A dark, quiet forge took up most of the back wall. The other three walls were covered in swords, daggers, and a variety of hunting traps. "He's quite the prolific craftsman for such a small village."

George stalked the length of the room. "I've heard of Hildaldo. He sells many of his wares to the local markets. I often receive requisition requests from the Ducal Guard stationed in Rothgart for his work." He halted mid-step, turning toward the right wall. "It's clear he's meticulous about caring for his forge. It might not seem in disarray to us, but he would have easily been able to spot something out of place." With that, George pointed to a bare spot on the wall. "A thin blade hung here. You can see the sunlight discoloration in the wood around it."

Jax gathered her skirts and stepped gingerly across the dirt floor, careful so as not to disturb any evidence left by the intruder. She arrived at George's side and stared at the blank space. "One of the stolen items?"

George nodded and moved a few paces down. "A trap hung here. Likely for small game."

From the opposite wall, Perry called out, "Looks like a knife is missing—a skinning knife, perhaps?" he guessed.

Jax counted the missing items thus far. "A thin sword, a hunting trap, and a knife. Looks like this 'ghost' is trying to keep themselves fed."

"Another hunting trap is missing." George frowned as he continued to scan the walls. "One, two, three, four…I count seven in total."

Perry folded his arms. "That's a lot of game to be hunting for one person."

Jax agreed with her fiancé. "Especially if they are already stealing food from the village."

"There's another possibility." George's features darkened. "Small game traps can serve another purpose: wounding a human."

Jax shuddered. Until now, the thief of Favored Crossing had seemed rather innocent, but George's comment painted a potentially darker picture.

"Yuryk mentioned he's sent scouts to check out the sounds coming from the ruins," Perry said. "Perhaps the culprit intends to ward off further visitors."

George's frown grew more severe as he studied the dirt floor. "Look at this." He summoned Jax and Perry to his side as he knelt closer to the ground. "You can plainly see the footprints we've left in the dirt."

"So?" Perry asked.

"So…ours are the only prints here."

Jax squinted, counting the shapes pressed into the earth. "You're right. If the culprit took these traps, he would have had to come this way."

Still keeping low to the ground, George began to move about the forge. Over by the entryway, he called, "I found the blacksmith's prints. From the looks of it, the blacksmith wears large work boots. It appears he stopped short of the threshold then hightailed it out of here."

Jax and Perry moved to the corners of the forge, diligently searching the dirt for any signs of disturbance. Other than their own footprints and those of the blacksmith, they found nothing.

"Could the thief have swept away their prints?" Jax surveyed the forge for a broom. She found one propped in the back corner by a small, unassuming back door. She hurried toward it, grabbing the handle, only to find it that it wouldn't budge.

A startled gasp came from the other side. "Is everything all right in there?" It was one of the Ducal Guard. Gunner Sampson, if she remembered the name correctly.

"Sergeant Sampson?" she said through a crack in the door. "Is there something propped against this door?"

"No, Your Grace," he answered quickly, "but there is a massive padlock."

"Has it been tampered with?"

A beat of shuffling passed before he replied. "No, Your Grace. No pick marks. Nothing."

Jax tapped her chin as she considered this information. She'd want to confirm her theory with either Yuryk or the blacksmith himself, but she wagered the blacksmith had swept his floor clean last night before leaving his forge through the back door and locking up.

A knock on one of the windowpanes startled her from her query. George moved to the window, slid back the latch, and pushed the panes outward.

"Well, that confirms it," a solider by the name of Carthield announced. "We've found no sign out here that anyone used the windows to enter, Captain."

George threw a quick look at Perry, who sprang into motion, checking each of the windows from the inside.

"All locked." Perry scratched his head, clearly puzzled.

Jax placed her hands on her hips. "So, both entrances to the forge were found locked and untampered with, and all the windows were latched from the inside." She shared a worried look with Perry and George. "Just how *did* our thief get in here?"

Her question hung in the air as an unsettling thought tickled the back of her mind. Maybe they *were* dealing with a phantom, after all.

Chapter Five

"There has to be a plausible explanation." George, ever the pragmatist, surveyed the scene again with a critical eye.

Perry, however, didn't look so sure. "I don't know, mate. The mysterious cries from the ruins suddenly make a whole lot more sense."

George shook his head and shot Jax an exasperated look, as if to say, *Please tell me you're not caught up in this phantom business, too.*

Jax didn't offer her opinion, and instead, strolled the length of the forge, examining the items laid out on the tables. Craftmaster Hildaldo kept mostly tools on display, each laid out perfectly straight, not a single one crooked or misaligned. It became very clear that the phantom burglar had not taken any of the items from the tables.

She suddenly stopped short, catching something that seemed out of place. A smudge of soot marred the corner of a table near the back of the workspace. Jax frowned. Everything else in the blacksmith's shop was in pristine condition, so why was there a smear on this tabletop? Jax moved on to the next table, and found another blotch of soot, this time between two hammers.

An idea began to take shape as she found more soot marks atop the tables. "Gentlemen, I don't think our 'ghost' used the ground to walk around." She pointed to a slightly more defined marking. "He used the tabletops."

Perry and George appeared on either side of her. "Good eye, Jax." Perry grinned in praise.

George's brow furrowed. "Indeed. That looks like a footprint to me. Smaller than the blacksmith's, for sure."

Jax's pride at having found the footprints was fleeting. "It still doesn't explain how our ghost entered the building." Her gaze trailed the length of the perimeter, flitting past the front door, the windows, the forge, the back door…before snapping her attention back to the forge. "Virtues! Is it possible they came down the chimney?" She rushed over to the massive forge, the only thing in the shop covered in blackened grime. She peered up the shaft that opened to the sky. "It's certainly wide enough for a person to squeeze through."

George was the first to join her. "Maybe a man of your size. I doubt Perry or I could fit." His lips curved into a scowl.

Perry poked his head into the shaft. "I'd have to agree; it would be a tight squeeze."

Jax pointed to the disturbed soot at the base of the hearth. "It's the only logical explanation. Our thief comes down the chimney, then uses the tabletops to move about the blacksmith's workspace." She tossed a pointed look at her companions. "Unless you'd seriously like to entertain the theory that a ghost passed through these very walls."

George ran a hand over his dark, close-cut hair. "There's nothing more for us to do here. I'm going to take some men and investigate the ruins while we still have some daylight."

"Wonderful," Jax said. "Just let me change into something more suitable, and Perry and I will come with you."

George's features turned steely. "No. *You* will remain here and visit your adoring public, Duchess. If the culprit *is* hiding out in the ruins, I can't risk you stumbling across one of those hunting traps."

Jax opened her mouth to protest, but Perry gently cupped her elbow. "Jax, I know your adventurous spirit is probably saying otherwise, but George is right. Let's spend this time with Favored Crossing. I need my fiancée in one piece."

She melted at his words. When it came to puzzles like the one before her now, she often forgot who she was and the duty she had to her people. Yet, the Duchess of Saphire couldn't rush headfirst into danger just to satisfy her curiosity. She had to put the needs of others before her own. "Yes, of course. You're both right." She shot a conciliatory look at George, who didn't quite meet her gaze.

Perry chuckled. "Imagine that, eh?" He ribbed George with an elbow. "Us, right."

George released a half-hearted laugh. "I'll escort you both to our campsite then take a squad of men to survey the ruins. With any luck, we'll ferret out the perpetrator by dinner."

‡

Jax's attention was diverted by shadows approaching the bonfire. Speaker Yuryk had been in the middle of an entertaining tale regarding a particularly rambunctious Yuletide feast when George and his men finally returned from their exploration.

The entire population of Favored Crossing fell silent as fifteen members of the Ducal Guard descended upon their jovial, lighthearted gathering.

Jax rose from the chair Speaker Yuryk insisted she use, rather than having her sit on the ground like many of the residents. "Any news, Captain?"

George shook his head, his face streaked with dirt and sweat. "Nothing among the ruins that we could find. However, Peter here—" he motioned to one of his soldiers "—found a beaten footpath in the woods southwest of the temple. The tracks have been washed away by recent rainfall, but the path is still worn." He directed his next question to Yuryk. "Do any of your people use that trail?"

Yuryk frowned. "No. Not many have reason to leave Favored Crossing. In fact, no one has left the village in recent weeks except my son. He was the one I sent to carry a message to Courtier Gavant about our troubles. But he took the main road." He pointed down the rough pathway Jax and her party had traveled earlier. "I don't know about this southwest trail."

"Then my men and I will investigate it further," George said. "With any luck, it will lead us to where the offender is hiding out."

Jax placed a hand on his forearm. "What about the ruins? Did you find any traces of our thief?"

"Not a thing. All we found is evidence of Yuryk's scouts."

"What about the moaning noises? Did you hear them?" Jax pressed.

George glanced to his men. "No one has inhabited those ruins for a long time, Duchess," he spoke to her formally in front of the crowd. "I'd wager some animal has been the cause of the unsettling noises. Bird calls can sound quite harrowing at times."

Yuryk bristled. "We've not been hearing bird calls, Captain." He practically spat the words out.

"I'm sorry, Speaker Yuryk." George sounded like he was struggling to remain calm and respectful. "But there is no evidence of any human activity among the ruins."

"That's because we're not dealing with a *human*, Captain. Virtues!" Yuryk threw his hands up in the air. "I thought you would help us, Duchess." Yuryk directed his frustration at Jax. "Not brush off our concerns and think us deluded."

Jax opened her mouth, stunned at the venom in his outburst. She wished George had approached the situation a little more tactfully, but diplomacy was her area of expertise, not his. "Captain Solomon meant no offense, Speaker. My men are doing their best to follow the evidence at their disposal." Jax could tell George did not appreciate her apologizing on his behalf, but he wisely kept his mouth shut. "Perhaps the solution to Favored Crossing's troubles will be at the end of this mysterious forest path."

Yuryk folded his arms, the jovial atmosphere of the evening gone. "I think it best if we say goodnight, Duchess."

Jax sighed inwardly, understanding the man's disappointment. "Your hospitality has been most appreciated, Speaker Yuryk. Lord Pettraud and I bid you and the people of Favored Crossing a good evening."

Perry jumped up from his own chair and hurried to her side, taking Jax's arm. Uma and Hendrie, who had joined them for the bonfire and storytelling, trailed after them, each wearing uneasy expressions.

"Are you sure it's safe to remain here, Jax?" Uma whispered once they were out of earshot of the grumbling crowd. "Yuryk looked awfully hostile."

"He's just upset about these thefts," Jax assured her.

"Nevertheless," George said with a growl as he strode beside Jax and Perry, "I'm going to assign some men to watch the perimeter of the hamlet whilst I investigate the woods to the south. I don't want anyone sneaking into our campsite to demonstrate their dissatisfaction with us."

Jax stumbled at his words. "You're not going there now, are you? It's nearly nightfall."

George shrugged. "I think it best if we catch this crook and recover what was stolen before we depart for Rothgart. Otherwise, a sour taste will be left by our visit."

By now, they had reached their encampment. Jax's tent, large enough for at least ten people, sat on the far side of the circle, guarded by two sentries.

"While I agree it's probably the best course of action," Jax said, "for Virtues' sake, do be careful roaming around in the dark."

"Always, Duchess." George dipped his chin. "I don't think I need to tell you all to be careful and on alert." His penetrating gaze met Uma's, Hendrie's, and Perry's before returning to her. "I can remain here if—"

"Nonsense." Jax waved away his concern. "You're one of the best trackers in the Ducal Guard. If anyone can chase down whoever used that path, it's you."

George placed something cool and slim in the palm of her hand. "Use this if you need me."

In the firelight flickering from the torches posted around their campsite, Jax could make out a shiny, silver whistle.

"All right, men." George straightened his shoulders and surveyed the assembled members of the Guard who were not on patrol. "Svenson, your group is still taking the night watch. Carthield, your column is with me. Peter, take us to where you found the trail."

Perry's arm snaked around Jax's waist as George and his men dissolved into the night. "They'll be all right," Perry assured Jax. "George will find the thief in no time."

Jax sent a prayer to the Virtues, hoping her fiancé was right.

Chapter Six

Jax awoke from her murky dreams with a start. As her eyes adjusted to the darkness saturating her tent, goosebumps prickled her arms before her brain could fully process what she was hearing.

A high-pitched, howling cry reverberated all around her, chilling her to her very core. It sounded childlike yet ancient at the same time—certainly not like any animal she'd ever encountered.

Fueled by adrenaline and a thirst for knowledge, Jax scrambled from the cot Uma had assembled for her earlier and raced toward the slip of light pouring in from the tent flap.

"W-what is that?" Uma murmured sleepily from her own bed.

Jax could barely make out her friend in the darkness. "I'm not sure, dear one. Stay put." With that, Jax poked her head out of her tent.

Two members of the Ducal Guard stood alert on either side of her, spears in hand as they surveyed the surrounding clearing.

"Sergeant Greene," Jax hissed to the taller of the two, "is that what I think it is?"

Light from their encampment's bonfire flickered shadows across the man's chiseled, tense face. "It's coming from the west."

"The ruins?" Jax studied the forest that encircled them. "Are you sending a patrol to investigate?"

Greene shook his head. "No, Your Grace. Captain Solomon and

his team have yet to return. Our duty is to protect you, and you alone."

Jax frowned. "But whatever is haunting the ruins is on the prowl *now*."

Greene raised an incredulous brow at his Duchess. "*Haunting*? Your Grace, surely you don't believe—"

"I don't know what to believe," Jax cut the man off. She immediately regretted unleashing her annoyance on him. Sergeant Greene was just following orders that, if disobeyed, could result in disastrous consequences.

The melancholy shriek penetrated the air around them once again. Alarm prickled at Jax's brain as unease wormed its way through her.

Private Doogal, Greene's partner, shuddered. "It sounds almost…otherworldly," he murmured, more to himself than to either Greene or Jax.

"Hush, Doogal. That's enough." Sergeant Greene reprimanded his subordinate. To Jax, he said, "Duchess, I suggest you try to get some sleep. No harm will come to you whilst we draw breath."

Jax knew she was being politely dismissed. She drew back into her tent, closing the flap.

"What's that terrible sound?" Uma's voice trembled from her side of the tent.

Jax fumbled her way through the dark, her knee colliding with her cot. "It's coming from the ruins."

"I've never heard anything so ghastly before." Her friend issued a quiet whimper.

"Neither have I." Jax peered through the darkness. "Uma, what if the people of Favored Crossing are right?"

"Right about what? That they're being haunted by a ghost?" Jax could plainly hear her friend's incredulity. "You're beginning to sound like Hendrie. He almost had me believing in spirits before we all retired to bed. But…I'm sure it's just some animal we've never encountered, Jax. Try to get some sleep. I'm sure the Ducal Guard will find its source."

The howling cry sliced through the night, sinister and low.

Jax balled her sheets in her fists. Favored Crossing was losing sleep night after night listening to these ghostly calls. Her people were suffering, and there was nothing she could do about it. The Ducal Guard stationed at her campsite couldn't leave their posts, and Virtues knew where the mysterious trail had taken George and his team. There was no one who could investigate the ruins, except…

"Jax? *What* are you doing?" Uma asked, perturbed. "I can hear you moving around."

Indeed, Jax was waving her arms wildly around the base of her cot. "Trying to find my boots."

"What in the Virtues do you need your boots for?" Uma hissed, keeping their conversation private from the men standing watch outside their tent.

Jax threw a pointed glare into the darkness, hoping Uma could see and feel the severity of her gaze. "*Someone* needs to investigate that sound."

"And you think the Duchess of Saphire is the right person for the job?"

"The Duchess of Saphire is *always* the right person for the job." A sly grin curled on Jax's lips.

Uma released an exasperated sigh. "You've gone mad. I mean, putting yourself in the path of murderers is one thing, but this is a whole other level of…well, quite frankly, stupidity."

Jax nearly burst out laughing. If someone had told her a year ago Uma Dorrow would have the spirit to stand up to her in such a brass manner, well, Jax wouldn't have believed them. Uma's audacious comment oddly warmed her heart. Their friendship had developed deeply since Jax had ascended the throne. She knew Uma only spoke from a place of love and concern.

"Dear one," she addressed Uma with a sigh, "the people of Favored Crossing are depending on us, on me, to resolve this issue for them. I am their Duchess; I'm supposed to protect them."

"Jax," Uma's response was deadpan, "no one in that village is expecting *you* to go traipsing about into the night, on the hunt for some ghost. George can send some men to investigate upon his return. He might be there now, for all we know."

Jax finally found her boots tucked under the cot. "If George is already there, I'll just confirm it and come right back."

"And how do you plan to visit these ruins in the first place? Do you think the Ducal Guard is just going to let you walk away from this camp without a fuss?" Uma's sarcasm whipped through the tent.

Jax felt around her cot again and found her cloak lying across the foot of the bed. She tossed it over her shoulders, hiding her nightdress from view. She then moved stealthily to the back of the tent, running her fingers underneath the material that skirted the earthy ground. "What they don't know won't hurt them." She waited, counting the seconds as they ticked by. A shadow passed over the back wall of the tent moments later. It was one of the Ducal Guard patrolling the perimeter of the campsite. She'd have to stay completely quiet and keep out of his sight for this to work. "Cover for me, dear one."

And with that, Jax scurried out from under the tent, plunging noiselessly into the forest underbrush.

Chapter Seven

Jax knew she was being reckless. If George arrived back at their campsite to find her gone from her tent without an escort, heads would roll…and hers would be one of them. Uma's chastising of her foolishness echoed in her ears, momentarily drowning out the haunting, screeching cry from the west. Jax's stubbornness had a habit of getting her into tricky situations. She would not let the people of Favored Crossing down, but she knew she had a duty to protect herself. As the last of the Xavier bloodline with no heir of her own, Jax had to keep the well-being of the entire duchy in mind, which was why she now skirted along the perimeter of the clearing toward the tent where Perry slept. Perry was forever reminding her and George that he was a "Knight of Pettraud, after all," perfectly capable of keeping Jax safe if the need arose. Well, now was the time for her fiancé to prove himself. While Jax was more than capable of taking care of herself, she figured she'd be in less hot water with George if she took a bodyguard along on this impromptu adventure.

Jax approached the back of the tent Perry and Hendrie shared, keeping a careful watch out for the sentries stationed around the encampment. She had less than a minute before the lad circling the perimeter completed his rounds.

In a smooth motion, Jax's fingers curled around the bottom fabric of the tent, and she lifted it an inch from the ground. "Perry, are you awake? It's Jax," she whispered, knowing guards stood watch at the tent's entrance, like they did at her own.

Perry's voice was closer than she expected. "I was wondering when you'd show up."

Despite the tension, Jax's lips curled into a gleeful smile. Perry understood her all too well. He knew she couldn't pass up a good mystery, and once again, Jax counted her blessings that he was to be her husband.

In the moonlight, Perry's head of dark curls spilled out from under the back wall of the tent. "I take it we're not going for a romantic stroll?"

"Who says hunting ghosts isn't romantic?" Jax teased as he climbed free of the tent. "Hendrie will cover for you?"

Perry let out a light snort. "Hendrie isn't even awake. That chap can sleep through anything."

Jax suppressed a snort of her own. "Come on, we can talk more once we've cleared the site." Jax tugged Perry into the dense, dark forest that cocooned the Saphire encampment and pulled him behind a trunk of a large tree. Not ten seconds later did the patrolman pass by their hiding place.

Shadows settled all around them, the forest illuminated by the fire flickering from the heart of the camp. Jax allowed her eyes to adjust, knowing they couldn't risk lighting a torch and being spotted.

"The moonlight is having a hard time penetrating the canopy," Perry murmured. Jax could just barely see the glint of his lavender eyes as he gazed upward.

She tried to catch a glimpse of the night sky. "Do you know which way is west?"

"I can't see the stars at the moment, so I guess we'll just have to follow our ears." Perry's fingers curled around hers. "This is incredibly irresponsible, Jax. You know that, right?"

"Come on, dearest. How many times in life do you get the chance to meet a ghost?" Jax nudged her fiancé in the arm.

"Oh, so it *is* a ghost now?"

"How else do you describe that—that sound?"

A light chuckle escaped him. "Between you and Hendrie…"

She pulled him forward, using her free hand to navigate through the trees. "This wailing nonsense is tormenting the people of Favored Crossing. I have to help them."

Perry pulled her hand upward, and soon, she felt his cool lips press against her skin. "Then I am here for you, darling."

She glanced over her shoulder, hoping Perry could feel, through the darkness, the love she felt for him.

Another piercing cry shattered the air, making the hairs on the back of Jax's neck go rigid. "This way."

They continued moving about the dark forest, patches of moonlight serving as their only source of guiding comfort. More than once, they stumbled, but they had at least made it far enough from the campsite to avoid detection from the Ducal Guard. The haunting moan served as an eerie beacon, growing louder each time it sliced through the night. Jax tried to figure out if there was a pattern to the timing of the call, but she could not detect one.

At least five minutes had passed since the last howling cry when the forest began to thin around them, and Jax could make out a moonlit meadow up ahead. "I think we're getting close to the ruins."

Perry dropped her hand, and a low ringing sound sang through the air as he pulled his sword free from its scabbard. "Our ghost has grown silent, but that might not mean much. Be on alert, Jax." He held his blade, poised at the ready, as they broke clear of the tree line and into the lush grasses shimmering in the moonlight.

"Virtues," Jax murmured in wonder at the sight before them. The meadow stretched out into the starry night, spanning at least ten acres. In the center of the smooth, verdant scene stood the remnants of what Jax assumed could only be a massive fortress. It was crumbled and decaying, but various parts of the ruin were still more intact than others. A collapsed archway twenty yards ahead of them signaled the entrance to the ancient temple. Some walls remained standing, but most of the citadel had eroded away, leaving behind large chunks of moss-covered rocks to prove its existence.

Perry whistled as he scanned the ruin. "I wasn't expecting this place to be so massive." He frowned deeply and shot her a wary, sidelong glance. "It's a lot of ground to cover."

Jax bobbed her head. "I didn't realize the Ancient Faith temples of old were so grand." The Faith in the Realm of Virtues today was very different than the Faith from centuries ago. For one thing, their temples were humble places of worship, not gaudy, opulent castles. Despite the ravages of time, it was clear this temple had once been an extravagant spectacle. "Let's get a bit closer."

Perry caught ahold of her wrist before she could take another step. "Are you certain we shouldn't wait for the Ducal Guard to arrive? I'm sure George heard the cries and is on his way."

"Oh, we absolutely *should* wait for them, but whether or not we *will*, is another story." With a wicked grin, Jax gathered her cloak and hurried toward the fortress, mindfully keeping an eye out for the blacksmith's missing hunting traps.

She practically felt the gust of wind that resulted from Perry's sigh. "At least I can say I tried."

Together, they crossed the overgrown meadow, heading toward the crumbling archway. Moonlight illuminated the scene around them well enough, but Jax dearly wished for a torch to light their path. It would be harder to navigate the ruins without a more concentrated light source.

She placed a palm on a large chunk of stone that had fallen just a few feet away from the entrance. Brushing away the moss and dirt that covered the rock, she discovered a carved, serene face underneath her fingertips.

"This must be a statue of one of the Faith's angels," she mused, pointing out the delicate artisanship to Perry.

A piercing wail jolted through the air, its proximity startling them both. Perry's arm encircled Jax's waist as he pulled her close. "Or one of its demons."

Chapter Eight

Jax playfully whacked Perry's chest before noting the seriousness of his expression.

"We really should return to the encampment, Jax."

She took his hand. "I promise we'll head back soon." She couldn't help but marvel at the history strewn across the ground. She'd never explored something so antiquated, from a bygone age before the Realm of Virtues was ever established. Her body hummed with anticipation at the thought of learning more. "I just want a look around."

Without waiting for her fiancé's reply, Jax stepped across the dilapidated threshold of the archway, visualizing the grand foyer that had once stood on the other side. Now, all she could see were crumbling walls set against the starry sky. "The cries came from the northern part of the ruins. Let's take a peek at the area."

Perry shook his head at her stubbornness, but did not protest further. He walked in step with her, his sword still at the ready. "What you hope to find, I have no idea. The townspeople and the Ducal Guard said they scoured the ruins and found nothing."

Jax stopped in her tracks at his comment. "You're right."

His shoulders sagged with relief. "Then we can head back?"

"No, Perry, think about it." Her heart began to hammer with excitement. "Everyone has been investigating the temple ruins, likely paying particular attention to the area where the wails were coming from." She snapped her fingers. "What if the ghost calls have been used to *divert* attention from somewhere else?"

Perry stroked his chin. "That would be a rather ingenious distraction."

She then tugged him in the opposite direction, toward the southern ramparts of the temple. "Ingenious, indeed." The mysterious howling had succeeded in frightening the people of Favored Crossing away from the ruins, but for what purpose, she did not know. "I wonder what this old sanctuary is hiding?"

Again, the eerie wail sliced through night, its prolonged cry sending shivers down Jax's spine. She buried her fear and continued leading Perry beyond the southern wall. "Might as well start here."

"What are we looking for, exactly?" Perry arched an eyebrow.

Jax shrugged. "Disturbed ground, I suppose. Signs of suspicious activity."

Perry used his sword to point to the tall grasses that had grown around the fallen debris. "Looks like the Ducal Guard has already investigated this area. I recognize these boot prints from the soldiers' sabatons."

"Then let's increase our search perimeter, farther from the main structure." She surveyed the meadow, spying a few large rocks southeast, near the tree line. *Maybe those are the remnants of a temple outbuilding,* Jax mused. "Why don't we start over there?" She pointed to the spot she'd been contemplating.

Together, Jax and Perry navigated away from the central ruins of the dilapidated temple toward their target. As they hiked, Jax wondered what this portion of the compound was used for. She didn't know much about the Ancient Faith's beliefs and practices, and she cursed her ignorance. It would be helpful to have a greater understanding of the temple's layout.

The shrieking cries had gone silent for now, and Jax basked in the fleeting peacefulness of the dazzling night. She could think more clearly without her mind being addled by the fear brought on by that otherworldly howling. Her practiced gaze continued to search the fallen debris all around them, hunting for the secrets this ruin contained. Rubble radiated out from the central structure. The debris must have come from the upper floors of the temple, having been dislodged or blown off by fierce winds. The glittering moon provided just enough light for Jax to see clearly, but she wished she'd had the opportunity to examine the ruin during the daytime.

They arrived at the small scattering of rocks in the southeast corner of the meadow. The ground here looked completely undisturbed. Jax swelled with confidence. She had been right. The scouts and the Ducal Guard had not investigated this far away from the main compound.

Perry dropped her hand and examined the largest of the old, ancient stones. "The craftmanship remains quite stunning after all this time."

Jax smiled knowingly at the twinkle in his eye; Perry had a deep love of art.

Her attention still on her fiancé, Jax stepped around a large rock, the size of a lumpy loaf of sweetbread, but her foot caught on something, and she stumbled forward. Jax cursed her clumsy footing. She thought she had missed the rock entirely, and when she assessed her boot, she found she was right. She hadn't tripped on the rock itself, but rather, a piece of rope snaking out from under it.

"Strange," Jax muttered. Unlike everything else surrounding them, the rope wasn't frayed or worn by age. She tugged on it, finding it pinned down by the bread-shaped rock. She curled her fingers around the rock and lifted, her knees buckling slightly at the weight.

Perry hurried to her side, sliding his sword back in its scabbard. "Need some help?"

"I've got it," Jax said through gritted teeth. She scooted the rock to the side, finding a loop of rope underneath.

Perry studied it alongside her. "Looks like some sort of handle."

"To what, I wonder." Jax reached for the rope and tugged.

The earth underneath her feet shifted, accompanied by a muted rattling sound.

Jax stepped to the side. "I think this is an entrance of some sort— a hidden route out of the temple." The Saphire palace, too, had several underground tunnels to spirit away the royal household, should the castle fall under attack.

Jax nudged Perry's side, silently asking him to move back. She, too, changed her position before giving the rope another tug.

This time, a large, square piece of overgrown grass and soil dislodged from the ground, moaning open to reveal a set of old stone steps that descended into the belly of the earth. As Jax tipped the trapdoor back further, the sod slid off, revealing aged but sturdy wooden slats, bringing to Jax's mind a rug covering a floor.

Perry scratched at his curls in wonder. "Well, I'll be. A secret entrance."

Jax craned her neck down into the passage. "It's too dark to see anything."

Her fiancé sighed. "What are my chances of persuading you to return to the encampment to share our findings with the Ducal Guard?"

Jax's pointed stare was answer enough.

"Well, then…give me a moment. Stay here, and do *not* move."

Eager to see what Perry had in mind, Jax nodded and propped the trapdoor open as her fiancé darted from her side, heading for the tree line.

He was back in less than a minute, holding several small branches, a large swatch of tree bark, and one large stick. "Could you, er, tear off a bit of your cloak or nightdress for me?"

Jax raised an eyebrow. "Why, Lord Pettraud!" she teased.

Perry's cheeks darkened in the unforgiving moonlight. "Please. When the time comes for *that*, I shall be the one removing your clothing, my darling."

His seductive words left her a little breathless as she scrambled to rip off a scrap of fabric from the hem of her nightgown. While her fingers fumbled with the linen, she watched out of the corner of her eye as Perry went to work rubbing sticks together in furious succession. "You're making a fire!" she exclaimed once she caught sight of smoky sparks.

Perry grinned as his curated flame burst into existence. "Quickly, the fabric." He waved his hand to hurry her.

With a hard yank, Jax tore away a long piece of her gown, handing it to Perry. He wrapped the fabric around the large stick he'd collected and began rubbing it across the back of the tree bark. "The sap will help the flame burn longer," he explained with a boyish grin. He then plunged the makeshift torch into the heart of the fire. It caught quickly, and soon, flickering light danced all around them.

"Impressive." Jax grinned as Perry stomped the ground, dousing the small fire as quickly as he had created it.

He handed her the torch, reaching once more to unsheathe his blade. "A Knight of Pettraud has many skills, Duchess."

"I look forward to making you use them all." Jax winked at her fiancé before gathering her skirts in one hand and taking her first step into the inky darkness.

Chapter Nine

Firelight danced along the old tunnel as Jax ran a hand over the cool stone. "It looks like this passage was carved into the bedrock." She admired the architectural feat, not realizing such construction was possible in the age before the Rebirth. "I wonder just how old this temple is."

In answer, Perry grabbed her elbow and yanked her back. "Watch your step!" The urgency in his hissed words frightened her.

Jax glanced down at the dirt ground. Her focus had been so enraptured by the design of the tunnel, she had almost walked right into the sharp teeth of a hunting trap. "Virtues." She shot Perry a grateful smile. "I guess our 'ghost' has put the stolen supplies from the blacksmith's shop to good use."

Her fiancé did not crack a grin. "You need to be more careful, darling," he said seriously.

Embarrassed by her near misstep, Jax shrugged off his reprimand and continued moving slowly along the tunnel. This time, she kept one eye on the ground while exploring her surroundings.

They came across another trap twenty yards further down the passage.

"Our ghost seems to not want any visitors," Perry murmured in her ear, his warm breath caressing her skin.

Jax examined the hunting trap a moment before continuing

onward. She puzzled over the strange scenario. "Someone has taken elaborate measures to secure these ruins. Scaring the villagers away and leaving traps…it all seems too resourceful for simple bandits." She paused a moment, lifting the torch to scan the walls around them. "I wonder if they're looking for something."

"Buried treasure, perhaps?" Perry's eyes widened with intrigue. "Left behind by the Ancient Faith of old?"

Jax nodded vaguely. "That's definitely a possibility, my love." Her keen gaze flickered ahead, noting a change in the tunnel's shape. "I think there's a small alcove up ahead."

With careful steps, Jax and Perry closed the distance, coming across a small nook just off the main passageway. All it contained was a large slab of rock that stood upright.

"If I had to guess," Perry said as he pushed back a lock of dark hair, "I'd say this is an altar of some sort."

Jax reached out and brushed a thin layer of filth from the stone. Her gaze narrowed as she studied her fingertips, which had collected little dirt. Someone must have recently cleaned this shrine.

The altar was smoother than the bedrock around them, and polished. She held the torchlight up to it for closer examination. The fire revealed swirls of white and gray stone. "This is marble." She straightened and studied the small alcove, wondering why the Ancient Faith had needed a shrine buried beneath the earth.

Her gaze roamed along the wall behind the altar, a flaw in the stone catching her eye. She moved forward for closer inspection, holding her torch as near as she could to the bedrock to banish away the shadows. "Perry, what does this look like to you?"

His muscular body pressed against her from behind as he leaned in to examine her findings. "Hmm, a carving of some sort. Of what, it's hard to make out." He reached out a hand and brushed away a coat of dirt that had caked onto the wall.

Jax squinted her eyes, willing herself to see the ancient carving more clearly.

"A crest, perhaps?" Perry began to trace the grooves in the stone. "Looks like this encompasses it all." He indicated with his fingers, which moved along a deep, engraved circle.

Jax scraped away more soil, this time using her fingernails. As the earth loosened and fell to the ground, a sharper picture began to form. "Why, this almost looks like a sun. See, these are the beams of light radiating from it."

"I can see what you mean. Maybe the insignia is depicting a sunset. These lumps could be hills." He motioned to the strange, ancient symbols carved into the stone.

"Or a sunrise." Jax shifted her attention to other areas of the wall. "I think there are more carvings." She found another circular emblem sculpted into the stone, but, unfortunately, even as she wiped away the dirt, she found the image to be horribly distorted. "It looks as though someone filed this one down." A frown grew on her lips. Initially, she had assumed their ghost to be the responsible party, but the longer she stared at the vandalized symbol, the more she realized the act had occurred long ago.

"I think there's another over here." Perry pointed to a spot on the other side of their sun crest.

Jax adjusted the torch to allow him to examine his find more closely. "Damn," Perry growled. "This one has been warped, as well."

She took a step back and studied the entire wall, wishing they had more light. She counted four insignias carved in a row. What did they mean? Were they some Ancient Faith ritual or an archaic way of telling time?

Her gaze drifted upward, above the four crests. She raised her torch to banish the lingering shadows. "Virtues!"

Her gasp echoed all around them.

"What is it?" Perry scrambled to her side.

Jax lifted her finger to a symbol inscribed into the bedrock above the others, a coat of arms she'd know anywhere. "That's the seal of House Xavier."

‡

What in the Virtues was her family crest doing down in these ruins? The question vexed her as she continued to stare at the insignia that her ancestor, Allonious Xavier, the first Duke of Saphire, had designed to represent his bloodline.

Perry released a low whistle. "I did not expect that."

"Neither did I." Jax's brow furrowed, her mind working furiously to figure out why the Xavier seal stared back at her from the decaying walls of an Ancient Faith temple.

A sharp wail ripped through the air, sending both Jax and Perry staggering back.

"That sounds awfully close," Perry whispered, reaching for Jax's arm.

Once her ears stopped ringing, Jax stepped back out into the main passage, suspicion fueling her onward. They hadn't heard the ghostly howls since they had discovered the trapdoor. What had caused the noise to erupt this time?

Leaving behind the puzzling shrine bearing her family crest, Jax motioned Perry to follow her. "The sound is coming from somewhere in this tunnel."

Sword in hand, Perry walked beside her, his expression pinched in concentration. Jax, too, listened for any indication that they might not be alone down here, but heard nothing emanating from the eerie darkness.

They had walked about fifty yards when Perry's arm shot out in front of her, forcing her to stop. This time, two hunting traps lay on the earthy ground. "We must be closing in on whatever these are meant to be guarding," he hissed.

Jax nodded at her fiancé's assessment, her stomach knotting with sudden unease. Her stubbornness and curiosity had gotten them this far, but now, fear finally was beginning to eat away at her. What had she gotten them into? Uma's reprimand echoed in her ears once more, and she dearly wished she had listened to her lady's maid.

Swallowing her anxiety, Jax forged ahead, Perry keeping in step with her as they navigated around the jaws of the hunting traps. Deep in her bones, Jax knew they were *this* close to finding out what was tormenting the people of Favored Crossing and why. She would not let fear deter her from helping her people.

Together, Jax and Perry quickly came upon a bend in the tunnel, each barely breathing.

Hand in hand, they rounded the passage, their mouths dropping open at the mystifying sight that awaited them.

Chapter Ten

Jax sucked in a breath as she inspected the contents of a large cavern.

Focused beams of moonlight bathed the center of the underground room, spilling in from a medium-sized opening in the domed ceiling. That, along with her torch, allowed her to make out a small cot tucked away on the far side of the room. There was a dormant campsite in the center of the chamber, and Jax guessed that the hole in the ceiling served as a rudimentary chimney if a fire needed to be lit. Fresh produce sat in wooden boxes, along with piles of clothing and linen.

"At least we can say we've uncovered the location of the goods stolen from Favored Crossing," she murmured, bemused at the strange sight.

Perry lowered his weapon an inch, one eyebrow raised. "Our ghost certainly requires a great deal of material necessities."

Jax hurried across the cavern toward the flimsy cot, eager to discover just who had been living down here. As she suspected, next to the pillow on the cot, she found some personal items belonging to their "ghost." A quill and ink, along with a stack of bound parchment, rested on the rock-hard ground alongside a cameo bearing the profile of a beautiful woman. A memento from the ghost's lover, perhaps?

Jax stroked the cameo and found it to be made of pearl. It was a high-quality trinket, for sure. Pearl cameos were usually only ever commissioned by those of noble or ducal blood.

While Perry inspected the campsite in the center of the room, Jax moved her attention to the stack of bound papers. At first glance, she assumed them to be love letters, but quickly realized her error. She skimmed the first page of the stack, her brain not making sense of what she read. It wasn't until she reached the document's end that she figured out it had to be written in code, for it was comprised of words she could not comprehend. After all, the continent had long been unified under one language, even before the Rebirth, back when the Ancient Faith still dominated the realm. Yes, certain areas of the continent had their own unique phrases and dialects, but the overall language was the same. So, whatever this was had to be written in code.

The next piece of parchment in the pile proved to be a crude, ancient map. Several water stains marred the charcoal etchings, but Jax could make out a few notable markers, one being Favored Crossing. She studied the map closely. Favored Crossing was so small and off the beaten path that it had almost escaped Jax's attention, yet she held an antiquated sketch of the settlement in her hands. She considered the map's importance. Favored Crossing had all but faded into obscurity, but it had once been important enough for someone to ink it onto parchment.

Her gaze darted over the remainder of the page, trying to decipher the landmarks through the smudges and water stains. Using the map's compass rose, she traced a finger to the west of Favored Crossing, to a darker smear on the paper. This spot had to indicate the temple ruins she stood under now. Holding the torch closer to the map, mindful of the hungry flames, Jax squinted. Were those X's inked across the remnants of the temple—

"Oy, get away from that!"

The harsh rebuke sent Jax jumping backward and dropping the stack of papers onto the cot. She whirled, following the direction of the cry, toward the threshold she and Perry had entered from.

A svelte finger stood in the archway, a thin sword gripped tightly in one hand.

Perry was beside Jax in an instant. "I warn you, do not come any closer."

The figure inched forward, stepping into the moonlight.

Jax sucked in a breath. Their ghost was a young woman, no older than twenty-five. Her copper skin shimmered in the ethereal moonlight, strands of gold glinting in her long burgundy-brown hair. She had a slender yet powerful form, and was undoubtedly skilled with the blade she wielded.

"An awfully bold remark to make, trespasser." Her voice was a rich, velvety growl.

Jax squared her shoulders and held her chin high. "*You* are the trespasser here."

The stranger took another step, now standing a mere fifteen feet away. "Is that so?"

Jax met the woman's arrogant gaze. "Yes. As Duchess of Saphire, these are *my* lands."

The stranger stilled, her dark eyes widening in disbelief. "Impossible."

"I think not." Jax lifted her arm, allowing the torchlight to wash over her, revealing the truth in her amethyst gaze.

The sword trembled slightly in the stranger's grip. "What is the Duchess of Saphire doing here?" Her lilting accent was unmistakably Hestian.

"Who are you?" Jax asked instead, ignoring the woman's penetrating gaze. What was someone from the southern duchy of Hestes doing holed away in an old Ancient Faith ruin in Saphire?

"My name is Emeraude, Your Grace," the woman replied with a dip of her chin. "Emeraude Odaire."

The simple, reverent action brought a slight smirk to Jax's lips. At least the 'ghost' of Favored Crossing was well-mannered. "And what brings you to my duchy, Mistress Odaire?"

A calculated grin curled on Emeraude's graceful face. "You still haven't answered *my* question, Duchess." She arched an elegant eyebrow.

"Excuse you," Perry said through gritted teeth. "*You* are not in a position to be asking questions, thief."

Emeraude's gaze flitted to Perry momentarily before settling back on Jax.

Jax did not like what she saw in that instance. Emeraude seemed almost amused by Perry's bravado. Unease clawed up her spine; this woman was dangerous. "The people of Favored Crossing asked for my assistance in ridding the hamlet of its resident *phantom*." Jax summoned all her poise and courage into a tight, severe mask. She could not let Emeraude know how nervous she made her.

A musical chuckle floated over the mysterious woman's lips. "I suppose I should feel honored, then? To be unmasked by a Duchess?"

"What are you doing here? Why are you tormenting Favored Crossing?" Jax pressed her quarry.

Emeraude's sharp, beautiful features darkened. "My business is my own, Duchess."

"When your actions affect my people, it becomes *my* business." Jax said with a slight snarl, puffing her chest.

"I see." Emeraude's expression grew pensive. "I take it you have been accompanied here by the Ducal Guard?" she drawled, shooting a dispassionate glance at Perry. "This man is hardly worthy to be your only escort."

"Now, see here!" Perry stepped forward, leveling his sword at the brazen woman's neck. "The Virtues will abandon us before I let any harm come to Duchess Xavier."

Emeraude's eyes brightened, two orbs flashing in the moonlight. "Xavier? Yes…Virtues, how could I be so foolish?"

Jax and Perry shared a quick, confused look. Mistress Odaire seemed to be talking to herself.

"Duchess Xavier, have you come to these ruins *only* at the behest of Favored Crossing?" Emeraude dropped the arm that wielded her slim sword, curiosity dancing across her face.

"Yes," Jax answered hesitantly. "We came to find the source of the haunting cries."

With her free hand, Emeraude reached for her side, pulling at something tucked in her belt.

For a harrowing heartbeat, Jax thought she was reaching for a dagger or short sword, but grew even more confused when Emeraude held the item out in the moonlight.

It was a hollowed-out piece of wood, a little more than a foot long. It reminded Jax of a broken oar handle.

"This is a sorrowflute. It was once used long ago in funeral rituals among the Hestian people in the days before the Rebirth." Emeraude flipped the strange instrumental in her hand.

Jax studied the strange flute with great interest. "You've been using *this* to create those terrifying noises?" She shuddered, remembering the gruesome wails. No wonder the rituals had since died out, what with the creation of dignified trumpets and horns.

Emeraude waved to the chamber around them. "There are tunnels throughout this ruin. I simply played the sorrowflute through the vents, much like the one above." She pointed to the circular hole in the chamber ceiling.

"Why?" Jax tilted her head. "This temple has been abandoned for centuries. Why make the villagers believe it was haunted?"

Emeraude shrugged. "I needed to make sure I wasn't disturbed." She folded her arms, looking both Jax and Perry up and down. "It seems my plan had the opposite effect."

"Disturbed from doing what?" Jax pushed.

"Your only interest in this place is me, Duchess?" Emeraude countered, her eyes glowing with a strange fervor. "Nothing else brought you here?"

Jax startled at the strange question. "I didn't know of this temple's existence until the people of Favored Crossing told us about it." She saw no reason to let Emeraude know why else her interest in this place had been piqued. Jax still couldn't shake her misgivings over finding the Xavier crest carved into the tunnel walls. Its presence among Ancient Faith ruins had left her quite unnerved.

Emeraude's lips twitched into a frown. "Hmm. That complicates matters."

Before Jax could press further, a deep voice echoed from the tunnel's darkness. "Jax! Perry! Where are you?"

Jax's heart caught in her throat. *George!*

Before either Perry or Jax could react, Emeraude lunged forward. Perry yanked Jax away before either of them realized that Emeraude was not coming for her, but racing toward the rickety cot. In one sweeping action, she collected her bound papers and sprinted toward the back of the chamber.

Emeraude paused at the edge of a long shadow, turning to meet Jax's astonished, questioning gaze. "When we meet again, Duchess,

I hope you'll be of more help." With that, she melted into the darkness, her footfalls going silent.

Overcoming their shock, Perry and Jax ran to follow Emeraude, finding a gap in the stonewall just big enough for the slender woman to fit through. Jax took a deep breath, ready to pursue, when a horde of footsteps announced the arrival of the Saphire Ducal Guard.

"Just what in the bloody Virtues do you think you're doing?" George roared as he stormed into the cavern. His unruly words rattled around the chamber.

Jax shrank back at the fury in his eyes. Normally, George kept his familiarity in check around his men, but her antics tonight clearly had driven him past his limits.

He stopped a foot in front of her and Perry, his normally warm chocolate eyes near-black. "Explain yourselves."

Perry's swallow was audible as he winced under George's fierce stare.

Jax, however, regained her composure, plastering an innocent smile on her face. "Just a little ghost hunting, Captain."

Chapter Eleven

George didn't speak to her the entire walk back to the campsite, instead directing his questions and comments toward Perry. She rolled her eyes at his childish behavior before cringing at the irony. Of all people, *she* had behaved childishly, putting both Perry and her in needless danger just for the thrill of a mystery. And what did she have to show for it? Nothing. Except more questions.

After Perry and Jax relayed their encounter with the mysterious Emeraude Odaire to George, he'd sent men to scour the network of passages than ran underneath the ancient ruins. Their search had turned up nothing besides more goods that had been stolen from Favored Crossing. Wherever Emeraude had escaped to, she had done so without leaving a trace.

"How did you know where to find us?" Perry asked, trying to play the role of mediator. George still wasn't speaking to Jax, and she had no desire to speak to him after the dressing down he'd given her in front of his men.

George answered curtly. "When the trail south hit the Beautraudian border, I knew we had to turn back. If the culprit escaped into the wilds of Beautraud, he was no longer under our jurisdiction. We had just returned to our encampment when we heard wailing coming from the ruins. I stopped by Jax's tent to report our findings, only to find a distressed Uma." His frown deepened.

"Despite her attempts to make excuses for Jax's absence, I guessed rather quickly where our ever-so sensible Duchess had gone off to."

Jax glowered at George's flippant remark. She didn't appreciate him repeatedly bringing to light the foolishness of her actions. However, affection swelled within her that dear Uma had at least tried to cover for her. Virtues bless her.

"We scoured the ruins upon our arrival," George continued, "and found your footprints leading away from the scene."

Perry ran a hand through his curls. "Jax figured out the strange cries were meant to lure focus to the temple, rather than to the area around it. A reverse diversion, if you will."

"How astute of her."

Jax's gaze narrowed as she finally made eye contact with her captain. About to berate him for his insubordination, her words died in her throat as she caught an impressed twinkle glittering in his dark eyes.

"Did you discover *why* such a diversion was needed?" George asked, his own curiosity etched into his piqued expression. "What purpose did this Emeraude Odaire have for being there?"

Regret and vexation flooded through Jax. "Our investigation into the matter was interrupted before we could find out."

George sighed. "Well, I'll send word to all our garrisons about this fugitive. If she intends to remain in Saphire, the Ducal Guard will find her."

Jax noted George's careful wording. Favored Crossing was incredibly close to the Beautraudian border. If Emeraude had escaped into the neighboring duchy, there was little more the Saphire Ducal Guard could do.

"Whoever she was, the woman seemed quite interested in your reason for investigating the ruins, don't you think?" Perry studied Jax with his lavender gaze.

Jax mulled over the strange questions Emeraude had boldly asked. "She did. Something about the Xavier name captivated her."

As silence settled over the group, Jax's curiosity continued to burn. Uncovering the mystery of the haunted temple had led to more questions. Why had her family crest been carved into the stone above an Ancient Faith altar? Just who was this elusive Emeraude Odaire?

Where had she gone? And more importantly, what had she been doing there in the first place?

Jax glanced over her shoulder, her amethyst gaze scanning the dark woodland that obscured the remnants of the ruined temple from view. *I wonder if we'll ever see her again.*

George cleared his throat, suddenly looking more contrite. "I'll send a team to reclaim all the stolen items once you and Perry are safe in your tents. Speaker Yuryk and his people will be most grateful to their fearless Duchess for banishing the phantom of Favored Crossing." He held her gaze. His apologetic expression conveyed a silent apology for his irate reaction to her midnight sleuthing adventures.

She placed a palm on his forearm as they strolled into the Saphire encampment, the warmth of the firelight washing over them. She couldn't fault George for his anger over her actions. She had behaved rather recklessly. What's more, Jax had seen a trace of hurt in George's eyes, as if he had been stung that she hadn't included him in her nighttime excursion. "Then my job here is done, Captain." Her soft, teasing words communicated her acceptance of his apology and issued one of her own.

"Thank the Virtues you've returned in one piece!"

Jax broke away from George's lingering gaze and turned to greet Uma just as her lady's maid enveloped her in a tight hug.

"You are in one piece, aren't you?" Uma held Jax at an arm's length, studying her up and down. "When I heard the wails grow more frequent then stop completely, I thought something terrible had happened to you."

Jax giggled. "We're fine, dear one. The only bruises I have are on my ego." She shot a sheepish glance at Perry and George. "We located the goods stolen from the villagers, but I'm afraid I have more questions now than I did before."

Uma's nose wrinkled. "Please don't tell me we'll need to prolong our stay here until you have these answers."

Jax heard both George and Perry suck in steeling breaths. "You know I love a good mystery, but I'm afraid I must turn my attention elsewhere for now." Jax gave a weak smile to her lady's maid. "There are more pressing issues in the realm for me to worry about than the motivations of a curious young woman."

"A woman?" Uma raised her eyebrows. "So, you met the 'ghost' of Favored Crossing?"

Jax threaded her arm through Uma's and headed for her tent, suddenly overwhelmed with exhaustion. "Let me tell you the harrowing tale."

‡

"We cannot thank you enough, Duchess Xavier." Speaker Yuryk bowed deeply, the gathered crowd behind him following suit. "Not only have you banished our phantom, but you have delivered our hard-earned goods to us as well."

Jax felt her cheeks warm at his reverent words. "The Ducal Guard returned what was stolen to you, Speaker." She motioned sagely to George and his men. "Lord Pettraud and I merely stumbled across them."

Yuryk turned to Perry. "The Virtues have blessed our illustrious Duchess with a suitor worthy of her strong nature. Lord Pettraud, the people of Favored Crossing are honored to have such a future Prince Consort."

Jax saw Perry shift on his feet beside her, clearly uncomfortable with the adoring attention.

George cleared his throat. "If this 'phantom' returns and gives you any trouble, send word to the Rothgart garrison, immediately. Help will come, Speaker Yuryk." His features tightened with the weight of his pledge.

"Thank you." The elderly man bowed once more before stepping aside, revealing the worn road out of Favored Crossing. "May the Virtues watch over you all on your travels."

As Jax took in the sight, she made a mental note to instruct her courtiers about the need for pathway restorations in this region of the duchy. If Favored Crossing was to flourish under her care, it would need smooth roadways to allow commerce to flow freely.

The Saphire delegation bid the villagers one final farewell and began their trek back to the ducal caravan. Bird song accompanied them, the woods surrounding their path no longer silent as they had been yesterday. Emeraude Odaire's sorrowflute must have frightened the wildlife away. Its return seemed a definite sign that Emeraude had left Favored Crossing behind for good.

Perry's fingers threaded through hers as the regal carriages came into view. "Are you sure you're ready to leave? It's not like you to give up on a puzzle."

A small sigh escaped Jax. Perry knew her too well. He knew this little adventure and its unanswered questions would eat away at the back of her mind. "I'm not giving up." She smiled at her handsome fiancé. "I'm sure I'll get my answers someday." As the Duchess of Saphire, though, she had more pressing matters to worry about at the moment—the political rebellion flourishing in Cetachi, for one.

As Perry helped Jax climb into their carriage, she tossed one last look down the road that led to the tiny hamlet, a place that had been all but forgotten by Saphire. She couldn't help but think that the Virtues had intervened and sent her to help the people of Favored Crossing. She shook her head wistfully, even as a grin unfurled from her lips. A ghost-hunting Duchess. What would she get herself into next?

With the mystery of Emeraude Odaire still churning in her mind, Jax sent a silent plea to the Virtues. *I do hope our paths will cross again.*

Will Jax come face-to-face with Emeraude Odaire again?

Only the Virtues know...

Murder is a royal affair.

Discover the Court of Mystery series on eBook, audio, & paperback.

The Court of Mystery series

The Ducal Detective
A Feast Most Foul
A Voyage of Vengeance
A Summit in Shadow
Throne of Threats
Paradise Plagued
Burdened Bloodline
Sovereign Sieged
Crown of Chaos
Harrowed Heir
Ravaged Reign
Innocence Imprisoned
Ardent Ascension
Eternal Empire

More Cozy Mysteries by Sarah

Trending Topic Mysteries
Glenmyre Whim Mysteries
Book Blogger Mysteries

www.saraheburr.com

Acknowledgments

Major thanks go out once again to Evan Grant for his review and comments, helping me stay true to the spirit of Jax and her friends.

I'd like to highlight the incredibly helpful work of Captain David Burr, who acted as my resident sailing expert, and although he was put off by my use of the words 'hallway' and 'room,' he was able to accept that this is a fantasy novel, so not all the sailing/boat elements are realistic within the world we know. His knowledge helped shape this adventure, and I thank him for his time.

Thank you to Tracy Lachowicz and Bettye Underwood for their copyedit and review.

Angelina Gennis, once again, mapped out the Realm of Virtues for my readers, this time putting her talents to use creating the *Rose of the Sea* schematic for the paperback edition.

I want to also thank Laura Burr for all the work she has done to help promote *The Ducal Detective* series throughout Mid-coast Maine.

A special thank you to Mihail Uvarov, the designer of the original series covers. Your depictions of Jax will always hold a special place in my heart.

Dedication

To a grand generation:

Paige and Betsy
David and Fran

About the Author

Sarah E. Burr has been dreaming of being Nancy Drew since her small-town days in Appleton, Maine—but when corporate America didn't deliver any mysteries, she started writing her own! Now an award-winning author, Sarah pens the Book Blogger Mysteries, Court of Mystery series, and the fan-favorite Trending Topic Mysteries and Glenmyre Whim Mysteries. Her cozy crafting caper, *You Can't Candle the Truth,* was a 2022 finalist for both the NGIBA and Silver Falchion awards, while *#TagMe for Murder* was a 2024 NGIBA finalist for Best Click Lit Fiction.

A proud Sisters in Crime member, Sarah also runs BookstaBundles, a content creation service for authors. She co-hosts *It's Bookish Time TV*, a cozy web channel full of fun author interviews, and blogs for *Writers Who Kill*.

When not plotting her next whodunit, Sarah sings show tunes, plays video games with her husband, and takes long walks with her adorable pup, Eevee. Want free short stories and exclusive updates? Join her newsletter here: https://bit.ly/saraheburrbookssignup.